A CHARMING DECEPTION

A Magical Cures Mystery

Southern Hospitality
with a Smidgen
of Homicide

Book Thirteen

BY
TONYA KAPPES

D1524048

TONYA KAPPES
WEEKLY NEWSLETTER

Want a behind-the-scenes journey of me as a writer?
The ups and downs, new deals, book sales, giveaways and more? I share it all!

As a special thank you for joining, you'll get an exclusive copy of my cross-over short story, *A CHARMING BLEND.* Go to Tonyakappes.com and click on subscribe in the upper right corner to join.

DEDICATIONS

I have to say that I'm so grateful for each and every one of y'all who have really loved this entire series! It literally changed my life over ten years ago. Not only did you make this a USA TODAY Bestselling series, you loved June Heal as much as I did.

June and the gang will always be my favorite series that I ever imagined. The fun of making up names, potions, and a spiritual world I'd love to live in myself has been a complete joy.

It's always sad to see a series end, but this isn't the last time you will see these characters! Be sure you're on my newsletter to be informed of where this cast of fun-loving spiritualists will be turning up again!

For now...I hope you enjoy your last trip to Whispering Falls.

Xoxo.
   T.

JUNE HEAL'S CHARMS

The List of June Heal's Charms and Meaning

- Turtle Charm = Be Sure and Steady on Your Journey
- Silver Owl = Wisdom, Mysticism, Secrets
- Purple Stone in Mesh = Clarity and Awareness
- Angel Wing = Guidance from Above and Protection
- Dove Sitting on a Gold Circle = Devotion and Hopefulness
- Third Eye Charm = Peer Past Illusions
- Small Potion Bottle = Harm to None
- Brass Bell = Brass helps protect from falling for the evil eye, from evil spirits and any sort of spell cast against you.
- Spiral Shape = Be aware of your surroundings
- Leaf = Stay true to you; listen closely to your intuition
- Elephant = God of luck, fortune, and protection and is a blessing upon all new projects.

CHAPTER ONE

"Good morning. Faith Mortimer here with today's *Whispering Falls Gazette* and your morning news."

I stopped putting the mojo bags I'd made for today's big summer sale for my shop on the display table to listen to today's newspaper.

No. It wasn't read out loud into our community over any loud-speaker. It was carried in the light summer morning breeze and was only heard by the spiritualists who had subscribed to our local newspaper.

It was only fitting that Faith Mortimer was the editor in chief since she was a clairaudient. It was her spiritual ability to hear things that were inaudible. She was able to hear beyond the natural sense of hearing.

In mortal speak, she could hear from spirits or angels or just hear into the future in some sort of mystical way I didn't understand since I didn't have that spiritual gift.

"As you know, our very own June Heal, owner of A Charming Cure, is going to be having our newest addition, and we are having a town-wide baby shower for our newest spiritualist. At least, we hope the new addition will be a spiritualist. Regardless, on Saturday, which is four days from now, we will be meeting at the gathering rock at midnight

during the peach moon phase to celebrate the arrival of Baby Heal...
um... or will it be Baby Park? No matter. June and Oscar Park are registered at Potions, Wands, and Beyond, located on the Hidden Hills: A
Spiritualist University campus located in the wheat fields behind the
gathering rock."

I rubbed my belly with one hand and Mr. Prince Charming with the
other, grinning from ear to ear about our little arrival. Though we
wouldn't be sure until the Little One was well into his or her teen years
whether there was some sort of spiritual gift, I would venture to say the
baby was, only for the fact that both Oscar and I were spiritualist. With
Oscar's being a wizard and my being a homeopathic spiritualist along
with my having a keen sense of intuition and dreams, there was so
much spiritual in our genes that there was no doubt our baby would
also be.

But there was one negative factor on my side. Darla, my mom,
wasn't a spiritualist, and that little percentage could affect my baby's
chance.

I casually flipped through the journal Darla had left me with advice,
potions, and recipes she had found helpful when she was trying to live
in a spiritualist world. I'd been looking for anything to do with her
being pregnant with me. The one thing I did find was how much she'd
loved the star-and-moon baby mobile my dad had brought home for
my crib. She'd even drawn a photo of it on the page. I wished she'd kept
it, but Darla wasn't about keeping things.

Darla was never one to keep any type of memories. She said that
the best memories were the ones stored in your head and heart, not
on paper or photographs. Though I wouldn't have minded a photo-
graph or two of us, a crayon drawing from preschool, or even a
report card that showed I was a straight-A student. Or something
from our time in Whispering Falls. But this drawing would have
to do.

My heart sank as I wondered if I could find any sort of mobile at
Potions, Wands, and Beyond.

Mr. Prince Charming was so good at hearing my thoughts. He

rubbed his body and curled his tail as though he were giving me a slight hug to let me know not to worry.

"I can't help it." I gave him one last rub before he jumped off the counter of my shop, A Charming Cure, and darted for the door. It was his way of letting me know it was almost time to open for the day.

"This announcement is brought to you by Wicked Good Bakery, the hosts of the shower. If you have any questions, you can stop by Wicked Good and see me or my sister Raven.

"In other news, we are having a summer sale for tourists starting this week. I hope everyone has made their sales signs and gotten their display windows already decorated for this morning's opening. If you've not noticed, the streets are already packed with tourists.

"Right now, we are also offering twenty-five percent off to any advertisers. Whisper to me in the air if you'd like some pricing."

I walked through the shop, straightening all the red tablecloths neatly laid on all the display tables that dotted the inside of the shop, and made my way to the front to make sure my shop window was ready just as Faith had asked us to do for the summer sale.

"Meowl, meowl." Mr. Prince Charming batted at the door.

"It's too early to open." I bent down and picked up a clump of his snow-white fur off the floor. "Are you feeling okay?" I gave him a good once-over when I saw the fur. "You never shed."

It was an observation I'd made very early in my life when I was ten years old and Mr. Prince Charming showed up on my childhood doorstep in my hometown of Locust Grove. It was also a reason Darla, my mother, who only liked to be called by her first name, even by me, had let Mr. Prince Charming in the house.

Or that was what I'd thought. Now I bet she knew he was sent by the Order of Elders and the Whispering Falls town council to keep a spiritual eye on me so they could see if I had any of Otto's, my father's, spiritual traits.

I did. And I was sure little Park would too. I rubbed the fur over my belly.

"Oh my. I think Little One loves you already." I beamed at Mr.

Prince Charming when the baby's foot followed the piece of his fur I'd dragged along my belly. "And to think I'm a little bit worried Little One won't be a spiritualist."

Mr. Prince Charming didn't seem to care as he continued to look at me and meow at the door.

"I'd prefer you not go out since the sidewalk is so full." I peeled back a corner of the display window that I hadn't yet opened so the tourists could see my display. "There's already a line."

Mr. Prince Charming wasn't going to settle down and let me get my work done so I could open up on time unless I let him out.

"Fine. But don't get into any trouble," I told him and opened the door just enough for him to slip out. "I hope you mind me better than he does." I rubbed my belly, talking to Little One, and walked over to the small table near the display window where I'd kept a small cauldron with warm tea for the customers to sip as well as a plate of cookies in the shape of my potion bottles, which I'd had especially made by Raven Mortimer from Wicked Good Bakery.

Even though I was a spiritualist, we were in the South, and we never forgot our Southern hospitality, especially since Whispering Falls wasn't your typical Southern town. Of course, the tourists had no idea we were spiritualists. They only knew how good they felt after shopping here all day, which made them want to come back even more.

We'd opened a subdivision up for non-spiritualists to live, but they couldn't open any stores here. We'd tried that once. *Once.*

With the tea-and-cookie station ready to go, I turned around to get a good look at my shop. All the display tables were filled with the various homeopathic cure bottles. Each side wall had display racks on the wall labeled with the various cures for what ailed them.

For instance, I had a display for gut health now that people were worried about health issues concerning their diets. The sleep display was by far my most popular. Everyone seemed to be sleep-deprived these days.

I rubbed my belly with a little smile, welcoming the nights Little One would have Oscar and me up.

I sucked in a deep breath, very satisfied with today's specials, which were written on the chalkboard near the far left of the shop next to the checkout counter. I gave the photo of my parents that hung on the wall a silent blessing and nodded to them before I turned my attention to the display window.

I'd opted for a summer theme, as the town council had strongly encouraged but hadn't told us to do. There was a red old-style bike with a nice vibrant white stripe and a white padded seat along with a picnic theme.

The red-and-white-checkered tablecloth on the floor matched the bike. I'd gotten a small red grill to sit on the edge of the tablecloth along with a brown picnic basket. There were a few sport items in the basket of the bike, representing summer activities.

To tie in what my shop was about, I'd added some homeopathic bug spray, citronella candles infused with a special touch, along with some various vitamins for the summer heat as well as some lotions for those aching bones and muscles that weren't used to being worked and overworked.

The final touch was the triangular banners made from various red-and-white patterned fabrics that hung all along the window. It was such a festive time of year for the mortals, and I wanted to capture the nostalgic feeling they seemed to have during these few months.

Even though I grew up as a mortal, summer was never my favorite time of the year. It was the fall—the early nights, the falling leaves, the moonlit skies, and of course, Halloween.

"It's time, Little One." I talked to my baby as though Little One was already here. "Here we go."

I pulled the cord to open the shades of the display window. The customers who were already standing in line oohed and aahed, making me smile in delight.

Before I flipped the front door sign to Open, I walked back behind the counter and around the partition where I kept my super-secret.

It was my cauldron, where the magic happened away from any mortal eyes. There were going to be a lot of potions made today, and with the fifteen-percent coupon on the total purchase I was handing out for the summer sale, I knew my cauldron needed to be nice and hot.

On my way toward the front door, I grabbed the white-and-red basket I'd found when I went to the flea market in Locust Grove after a doctor's appointment because I knew it'd be perfect for the color scheme I'd created for the display window. Inside were the coupons I'd had printed to give out to the customers today.

I took a deep breath and ran my free hand over my black short-sleeved shirt, tugging at the hem so it would flow down past the waist of my black calf-length A-line skirt. It was a perfect outfit for any pregnant spiritualist. I'd been able to score the cutest pair of low-heeled black lace-up boots at Potions, Wands, and Beyond when I went to visit my aunt Helena at Hidden Hall, a spiritualist university where she was the dean.

"Here we go, Little One." I tucked a piece of my short-bobbed black hair behind my ear and curled a smile on my face to give me the extra oomph to open the door. "Good morning," I greeted them and propped open the front door. "Welcome to A Charming Cure."

I gestured to the sign hanging in front of my small cottage shop.

"We've got plenty to go around and a sale coupon for you to use on your entire purchase today." I turned around and invited them to walk under the purple-and-white wisteria vine that grew up and around the front door of the shop.

It was a touch Darla had done when she owned A Dose of Darla in this exact same spot when I was a toddler. I couldn't wait to give Little One the same experience I had, only we would live in Whispering Falls our whole lives. Darla had to move after my father was killed in the line of duty as a police officer.

It was one of the spiritualist rules, and since Darla was not a spiritualist, only married to one and a mortal, she was unable to stay here. That was how she'd ended up opening the A Dose of Darla booth in the Locust Grove flea market.

"Welcome," I greeted the customers at the door and held the basket for them to take a coupon. "We have some wonderful hot tea and delicious cookies for you to enjoy while you look around."

My intuition keyed in on a young man. I could feel the itching inside of him. Though I hadn't gotten a clear picture of just what he needed, I did know he was my first potion customer of the day.

"Can I interest you in a cookie?" I asked.

"Thank you." He was probably in his midtwenties, and if I had to guess, I'd say he was with his grandmother.

"This is a fun one. Extra icing." I handed him one of the cookies decorated as a potion bottle filled with green icing. "Are you playing chauffeur today?" I asked when my fingertips barely touched his so I could get a sense of what he was all about.

CHAPTER TWO

"How did you know I was the chauffeur to my great-aunt today?" the young man asked and bit into the cookie.

"Great-aunt." My brow lifted at how wrong my senses of the grandmother figure were, though I knew she played a part in this situation somewhere.

Out of the corner of my eye, I saw one of the empty potion tin tubes on the shelf begin to glow a faint green, letting me know that was the tin tube for this particular customer. For some reason, the tin tubes were mostly for the men, while the ornamental bottles generally lit up for the women.

"I'm guessing you aren't here for bath products," I teased when I noticed his great-aunt checking out the bath bombs. "But I do have a line of men's products that might interest you."

The images of his hairline underneath his longer hair along his neck tapped into my intuition.

"I'm. . ." He casually shook his head no, but the green tin tube on the shelf lit up more, telling me yes.

"I have a lot of male customers who have very dry skin, kinda like eczema." I knew it was part of his problem, but truthfully, it was his obsession with sodas that made the pop fizzle of my intuition spark. "Do you experience dry skin in areas?"

"Yeah." His eyes popped open in a how-did-you-know kind of expression that I saw on a fairly regular basis when I was on the money about their ailments. "I get it in my hairline. My doctor gives me cream for it, but it rarely helps."

"I'm sure your doctor knows what they are doing, but why not try this." I had him follow me over to the men's section, though it was the exact same stuff I had in the women's section.

Men were so picky about that type of thing.

"Tell me if you like the feel of this cream. Too shiny? Too thick? Too sticky?" I grabbed the tin tube of cream off the shelf and unscrewed the lid. I put a dab of the cream on the back of his hand and waited for his reply.

I watched him rub it in and bring it up to his nose to smell. Another man thing was the perfume smell. What he didn't know was the creams in my shop took on the smell of things they liked. In his case, I could have sworn it smelled just like burnt marshmallows.

"This is actually really nice." He took the tin tube from my hand and looked at it. "Cream for Men. Huh." His brows furrowed.

"How about I give you a sample to take home. If you like it, you know exactly where to find me." I held up a finger. "I'll be right back with your sample."

The happy voices of other customers delighted my ears when I walked back to the counter to get the special lotion for the young man. I walked over to the shelf where the empty bottles and tubes were located and plucked his off the shelf.

"Do you have a question about the mojo bags?" I asked another customer when I noticed she was digging through them.

"Yes. I have some questions about them." She had picked up one of the red bags, which was worn around the wrist to help with the halt of gossip.

"Why don't you keep looking through them while I finish up with another customer. I'm sure we will be able to find the right bag for you,"

I assured her and walked behind the counter and around the partition to add exactly what was needed to the young man's cream.

Using my fingers, I carefully slid them up the tube and let the cream fall into the bubbling and murky contents of the cauldron. The cream swirled and mixed into the elixir. The steam pulsed up in ivory smoke as the smell of salt filled my lungs, leaving me with a taste of marshmallows and chocolate. Images of the young man sitting over a s'more maker across from a young woman popped like fireworks above the rim of the cauldron. Visions of him smiling, happy and exactly where he needed to be, reflected inside of the mixture as it moved in circular motions.

I turned around and grabbed galanga root from the ingredient shelf on the wall behind me. With a little pinch, I knew the young man would be able to heat up the relationship he wanted with the woman in my visions.

"This should do the trick for his itching." I took two laurel leaves and crushed them, using the cauldron stick to make sure they were coated in the mix, where they'd dissolve.

With a wave of my hand, I repeated the healing prayer twice. "Take care of his mind. Take care of his love. Take care of his emotions. Let life flow through him joyfully as he feels safe and relaxed."

The caldron shut off, letting me know his potion was ready to go back into the tube. I held the empty tube, which glowed as he talked to me over the cauldron. I had no idea how it did it, nor did I ever question it. Without my even noticing, the cream inside the cauldron had been moved into the tube along with the perfect label and instructions.

"I feel better already." The young man was standing at the register when I came out from behind the partition.

"I'm so glad." I rang up his total and added the coupon before exchanging money and the tube. "You let me know if you have any questions. I put a business card in the bag with our phone number on it."

"Thanks." He dangled the bag in the air, his spirit much lighter than when he first walked in.

His great-aunt came up to see what he'd gotten. "I bet this one will work," she told him.

My intuition went off when I realized she needed a light of some sort, a light within her that I wouldn't be able to provide with my shop, but I knew someone who could help her.

"Have you two been over to Mystic Lights?" I asked them about the lighting shop across the street, owned by my dear friend, Isadora Solstice.

They both shook their heads.

"I'm not sure if you're looking for any sort of lamps or lights, but she has the most incredible ones that you can't get anywhere else." I gently reached over near the register and tapped on what appeared to be a round light, and there was a peaceful blue glow that sprang to life.

"A touch light?" The great-aunt's face came to life. "Is Mystic Lights having a sale?"

"Here." I took one of the coupons from the basket. "You take this over there and tell Izzy that June sent you."

He and his great-aunt left without her buying anything from me, but that was how our magic worked. I knew she needed some internal work that I couldn't give her with my spiritual gift, but with my intuition, I knew my friend Izzy could.

Like I mentioned, Izzy owned Mystic Lights, a light-fixture shop that was a cover for her spiritual gift of crystallomancy, or as mortals would say, crystal ball gazing.

Izzy was able to use the art of future visions.

"Thank you." I wanted to give credit to Madame Torres, my crystal ball, for lighting up for the great-aunt when I tapped her.

Madame Torres was careful not to create much visual light, since it was how the mortals would see her. Since she was my crystal ball, only I could see her face or any sort of visions she might try to give me.

I wasn't a future reader or crystal ball reader for others like Izzy. It didn't work that way with the spiritual gift I had. In fact, Madame Torres had been waiting for me all her life until I'd walked into Mystic Lights for the first time several years ago, and when she appeared and I could see her, it was then that she knew I was her owner.

Sometimes I felt it was the other way around when she didn't show up exactly how I needed her to. But today, she'd worked like a charm.

"I'm sorry that took a little longer than I thought." I had gone back over to the customer with the red mojo bag. "I bet you just graduated from college."

She gasped. "How did you know?"

"I can see the pride written all over your face." I kept to myself the fact that I felt the tension knotted up in her about a job and that she was wondering if she was going to get the perfect one for her. That was why I decided to hand her the furculum mojo bag. "I would love you to have this."

I opened the small pink velvet pouch and dumped the contents into her palm.

"Is that a gold wishbone charm?" she asked as the excitement escalated in her veins. The pulsing was banging in my ears.

The Little One used both hands to drum on my belly as the young woman's excitement grew.

"It is." I left out the fact that it was a small turkey wishbone that made wishes, hopes, and dreams come true. "Along with a small green candle to burn while you take a bath and sprinkle the white rose petals in your water." I picked up the small vial of crushed petals. "I would suggest you head on over to my friend KJ. He owns Scented Swan Candle Company, the candle shop down on the left. He is giving away his specially made matches to any customer who receives a mojo bag."

"How much?" She dug into her purse.

"It's a graduation gift." My head tilted to the side, and my smile grew. Out of the corner of my eye, I could see Constance and Patience Karima scurrying to the side of the steps to let Mr. Prince Charming pass to enter my shop first.

The gray-haired older women were twins, and they were dressed in their usual house dresses. They looked around in unison until their eyes caught mine.

"Are you sure?" the young woman questioned me with tears in her eyes.

"Yes. I am sure." I needed her to leave before the Karima sisters reached us, especially Patience. I could see she had something in her arms that appeared to be dressed in a baby's dress.

We tried to keep the spiritual secret of our community on the down-low, and the Karimas were anything but down-low.

"Then I'll take it." The young woman smiled, and her tears began to dry.

"I know life can be challenging at your age, what with wondering whether you're going to get your foothold in the world with a job and all the other things piling up and throwing you into adulthood." I patted her arm, giving her a secret blessing. "I'm positive you're going to land your dream job."

I had no idea what her dream job was, but when I touched her, my intuition lit up with the proof I needed to confirm she was definitely going to be just fine.

"June," Constance Karima butted in between me and the customer. "June, have you decided who is going to babysit Little One?"

"Yes. Little One," Patience repeated in a very eerie voice, hoisting a sack of flour that was dressed in a little-girl dress up onto her chest.

"I'm going to go now." The customer was talking to me, but she was unable to take her eyes off the dressed flour.

"Please, let me know how it all works out for you." I pointed around the Karimas to the little satchel. "There are directions inside for you to follow. And don't hesitate to call the number on there if you have any questions."

The young woman got Patience's attention.

"What are you looking at?" Patience questioned then sniffed the young woman.

The poor girl did a little jerk before she scurried out the door.

"You can't come in here and scare my customers or sniff them." I moved them to the back of the shop, where I ushered them into the storage room behind the checkout counter. "Why don't we sit down."

The back walls of the storage room were lined with every ingredient that I had ever dreamed of. Bottle after bottle was in alphabetical order. The dried herbs hung from a clothesline around the room. There were burners, test tubes, melting pots, strainers, muslin cloths, cauldrons, and much more. There was a couch, a desk, and a mini-refrigerator that I kept stocked for the late nights I worked and needed a quick rest.

Lately, I'd been staying later due to the fact that I was trying to get as many products made up as possible so when I did have Little One, I'd be able to take maternity leave.

"You stand," Constance instructed Patience.

"Yes. Stand." She bounced the flour close to her.

"As you can see, we've been taking the arrival of the Little One very seriously." Constance pointed at Patience. "We've been carrying around the flour sack as though it were the Little One. Dressing it. Feeding it. Waking up in the middle of the night with it."

"And how does one do that with a sack of flour?" I questioned.

"One of our customers was a teacher, and she said they would give fake babies to children in the class to learn to care for a child." The Karima sisters owned Two Sisters and A Funeral, where they disguised their ghost whisperer spiritual gift.

"Your customer hasn't crossed over?" I questioned, thinking it was odd since that was what the Karimas were supposed to help them do.

"We feel like it's necessary for her to stay put until the Little One gets here." Constance reached up from where she was sitting on the couch and patted the bottom of the flour like it was a baby's bottom. "A little insurance so we know what we are to do when we watch the Little One."

"Insurance." Patience nodded with more bouncing force than needed. The seams of the flour sack were taut and made me worried it was going to explode all over my storage room.

"What type of insurance?" I asked, keeping an eye on the bag.

"We told her that she needed to help us learn to care for a baby, and then we'd let her know which door she needed to cross over into to make sure she sees her family that's passed before her."

Constance was blackmailing a ghost? I shook my head. "I don't believe this is how the whole afterworld works." I wasn't sure, but I believed God had more of a say of when someone left this earthly world, but I wasn't like everyone. "It seems you are blackmailing her."

We all had different beliefs, and my beliefs had been formed when I was younger and went to church with Oscar and his uncle Jordan.

Darla didn't take me to church. She was where I got my good spirit-filled soul and was taught about being good and doing good along with kindness and love.

I had rolled up all my beliefs in one and hoped for the best.

"Mm-hmm, blackmailing." Patience patted harder.

"She wakes us up in the middle of the night so that we are trained to hear Little One. She screams for food every few hours and has a different scream tone for potty." Constance spoke with conviction in her tone. "We are learning the ins and outs of being good caregivers for Little One, since we had no children of our own."

"No." Patience changed her patting to rocking back and forth on her thick-soled black shoes. "No children."

"But Little One, dear sister." Constance looked over at Patience with a smile.

"Yes, seester, Little One." She grinned, pushing her glasses up a little farther on her nose.

"So we'd like to know. . ." Constance started to say.

"There you are." Oscar Park, my husband, poked his head in the door. "Faith is out here, ready to take over. Hey, sisters." He gave them that big bright smile, causing both the sisters to blush. He looked at his watch. "We are going to be late. Are you ready?"

"More than you know." My eyes widened secretly, telling him just how much he'd saved me from making any sort of commitment to the Karima sisters about babysitting Little One.

"What you got there?" Oscar asked Patience.

"Little One." She grinned and flung the sack onto her shoulder, tapping it like she was burping it.

"Oh." Oscar's eyes grew wider, shifting to the left to look at me. "Let's go."

"June, dear, we will revisit this later," Constance called out to me after Oscar took me by the hand to drag me out of there.

"Close call," I whispered and grabbed my purse, which was hanging on the back of the stool that was behind the counter, where Mr. Prince Charming was curled up and sleeping. "Are you going?" I asked him, but he barely looked up at me. "You can rest." I ran my hand down his fur, trying to get a sense of what was going on with him, but nothing came through.

Faith was already working with a customer, and I didn't disturb her. She glanced over with her big onyx eyes, making eye contact and smiling. Faith always worked for me when I had something that kept me away from working. Other than that, I loved being in A Charming Cure. She had her long blond hair pulled back at the nape of her neck with the apron tied across the back.

"I'm worried about Mr. Prince Charming," I told Oscar on our way out of the shop. "He lost a clump of fur."

Oscar had the green machine parked in front of the shop. He held the passenger door open for me. His hand brushed up against my belly, and Little One moved.

"Oh. Dance party." I looked down and watched as my belly moved around. Oscar put his hand on my stomach. "Little One knows Daddy."

"I love you so much." Oscar had bent down and talked to my stomach like we'd learned from all the baby books we'd already devoured. He moved his mouth up to mine. "I love you so much too."

Gingerly, he kissed me then lovingly stared into my eyes.

"You're going to be a wonderful mother." His words put a little electric shock to my heart, bringing up some deep-rooted fear I'd always had about being a mom.

When our relationship had turned to much more than a friendship and progressed to the stage where I knew we were going to be married, I let Oscar know I wasn't sure I wanted to have children.

It wasn't a selfish act. I knew how hard it was for Darla to raise me after my father had been killed in the line of duty. I remembered all the birthday cakes from the grocery that were a day old and had someone else's name on them and weren't picked up. And I remembered the manager-special meat that was a day old. Trust me, Darla kept me in secondhand clothes and food on the table, and she loved me unconditionally, and at the time, I had not been schooled on the ways of the world.

Not that I was resentful to her, but I knew Oscar's job as a police officer wasn't always safe, and I certainly didn't want to have that kind of life repeated for my child. I believed all things happened for a reason.

When I found out I was pregnant and not with a constant flu, we were surprised and maybe shocked. But I knew this was the right path in our life, and we were very excited.

"How has your day been?" I asked Oscar and took in the beautiful backdrop of Whispering Falls.

The old El Camino crept down the main street. Almost everyone on the sidewalks took time to stop what they were doing and wave at us. The town was warm, welcoming, and charming. It was the perfect place to raise Little One.

Whispering Falls was carved into the side of a mountain. The moss-covered cottage shops were nestled deep in the woods and had the most beautiful entrances with their colorful awnings, displaying the shop names over the ornamental gated doors. It had a magical feel. And magic was how the town was built.

"It's been good. No crime to report." He kept both hands on the wheel and drove slowly around the curvy road. It normally took about twenty minutes to get to Locust Grove, but with his speed, it would take us double the time.

"You'd better hurry it up," I groaned from the passenger seat and looked at the old wooden sign that marked the end of Whispering Falls.

"Welcome to Whispering Falls, a Charming Village," read the old beat-up wooden sign. It took me back to the first time I'd ever seen it so many years ago.

"You know, I'm excited Little One will be growing up here and not in the mortal town."

Oscar's remark caught me off guard. "Oh yeah?" I questioned. "I think you and I had a wonderful time growing up next door to each other. I'm worried Little One won't have any friends to play with."

"I've been thinking." Oscar glanced over at me. "Gosh, you're glowing." The love he had for me was written so deep in his eyes that it pierced my soul, making Little One go nuts.

"Our baby feels our love." I put my hand on my stomach. "And we are curious to what has you thinking."

"Well, your aunt Helena came to see me today."

"And she didn't stop by to see us?" I referred to Little One and me, thinking how unusual it was for her not to literally twirl in and out of nowhere.

"She felt like she needed to talk to me about childcare because she's been hearing rumblings of how everyone is wanting to care for our Little One."

He was right. Everyone had offered their services to keep the baby when no one had even asked if we had a plan.

"Let me guess. She has a plan." I didn't have to guess to know she did.

"She actually has a great plan." Oscar and I had wondered what we were going to do but never really worried about it.

It wasn't like I couldn't take Little One to work with me in the beginning, but once Little One started to crawl or move around, it would not be safe in a shop with glass bottles everywhere.

"You know I don't want to shield the baby from our life. I would like to make sure our spiritual world is always present. Not how I or you were raised." My voice cracked. Immediately, I put my hand on my stomach when I felt nothing move.

"What's wrong?" Oscar could always tell when something was not right with me.

"The baby has stopped moving." I tried to blink away the worry. "The baby never stops moving."

"I'm sure it's all fine." Oscar smiled. "We all get worn out. There's not much more room in there for Little One to move around in." He reached over and rubbed a hard palm across my stomach. "But you're right. We don't want our baby to grow up and not know our heritage."

He slowed the car down as we passed our childhood homes in Locust Grove. We'd lived across the street from each other and relied on our friendship to get us through.

"That's why I really like Aunt Helena's suggestion." He took his hand off my stomach and kept his eyes on the road as we made our way through the busy streets of Locust Grove to get to our doctor appointment in time. "She suggested using the childcare center located in Hidden Hall."

"All the way over there?" My jaw dropped at the thought of Little One not being within a minute of me.

"June, let's be reasonable and work this out." I didn't like his tone of voice.

"Reasonable?" I gasped. "I'm nothing but reasonable when it comes to our baby. Common sense is above reasonable."

"Then hear me out." He had a point. "Honestly, it takes all of five to ten minutes to get to the wheat field where the portal for Hidden Hall is located. Then it's a simple walk through the university to get to the daycare center where all the spiritualist teachers' kids and some of the students' kids go. Little One will be around children with different gifts and talents, unlike you and me, where we knew something was different about us and thought it was the sugary Ding Dong." He pointed at the glove box.

"You didn't." My mouth started to water. I opened the glove box to find a few foiled Ding Dongs in there, waiting to be devoured.

"I knew you'd need one or three after I told you about how I thought Aunt Helena had a good suggestion." He was pretty proud of his sneakiness to sweeten up the offer with my go-to stress reliever.

Ding Dongs, though sugary and chocolaty, were my favorite food group. They helped me escape into my thoughts with reason and calmness better than any potion I could make for myself.

While Oscar continued to make a case for Little One to go off to daycare, I enjoyed the mouthwatering treat.

"We don't have a lot of time to make decisions." Oscar had a countdown to the due date for Little One.

"Remember what the doctor said about how first-time moms generally go past their due date?" I had to keep referring back to the doctor and the basics of childbirth when it came to Oscar's deadlines.

"You remember this isn't just any baby." He turned the green machine into the parking lot and pulled up to the front door of the doctor's office then shoved the gear shift into park. He jumped out and went around the front of the car to open my door.

I took his offered hand to help me out.

"This is *our* baby," he finished and hurried over to open the front door of the building. "I'll meet you inside."

I walked through the door and turned around to watch Oscar hop back into the car to find a parking space.

"You are in for it, kid." I rubbed my belly and turned to walk down the hall. "If he's this nuts about your safety while you're in my belly, he's going to drive himself crazy when you're toddling around."

"Your husband too?" a voice came out of nowhere.

"I'm sorry." I laughed. "I seem to talk to myself a lot these days."

"I totally do too." The woman smiled and put her hand out. "Sylvia Long."

"June. Nice to meet you." I left off my last name. Even though I was legally a Park, with Oscar's last name, I still went by Heal. "How far along are you?" s

I didn't see a noticeable baby bump like my big beach ball.

"I'm not sure if I'm pregnant or not." She held her crossed fingers up in the air, sending my intuition off in a crazy direction.

The pain and anxious feelings coursing through her veins were like electricity running through my body. I could feel the tension of uncertainty and pricks of needles hitting me from all angles.

"I'm sorry." The words left my mouth, and we gave each other knowing looks. "How many miscarriages?"

"Seven if you count the four times the in vitro fertilization didn't take." Her brown eyes had a sadness deep in the hazel flecks. Her brown hair was curly and draped down her back, almost damp, as it was drying naturally. I got the notion that if she did dry her hair with a hair dryer, it would curl up even more. "Today we find out if the seventh IVG has taken."

We walked into the office at the same time and headed straight for the clipboard, where we did the same ritual as all the other patients who came here. Sign in, then go pee in a cup, only to come back out and thumb through magazines from ten years ago and realize you've already looked at them the million other times you've been there.

This time, it was refreshing to go through the motions and have someone to talk to, even though I tried to keep it positive when talking to Sylvia after I knew she wasn't with child.

"June Heal Park," the receptionist called my name after opening the door.

"It was nice to meet you," I told Sylvia and headed through the door. "My husband is still parking the car. Can you bring him back when you see him?"

"Of course." The young receptionist smiled and had me follow her down the hall. "Room four. And your insurance is Intuitive?"

"Yes. Dr. Sebastian has the card on file." I had no idea how Aunt Helena used spiritual insurance with mortal doctors, and I didn't ask or care. As long as Little One was delivered safe and sound, it was all good.

"Yes. I bet he does." She spoke with a sarcastic tone that set my intuition off like gongs.

"Thank you."

I walked into room four, where she had me sit down and took my vital signs. I put her snide comment in the back of my head, chalking it up to crazy hormones that made me cry one minute and offended the next.

"The doctor and nurse will be right in." She didn't give any signs that my vitals were off, which didn't set my intuition on fire, which was a much-welcomed thing right now because I was already exhausted, and

I still had the entire day ahead of me. She only gave me the usual instructions on how to get ready for the doctor's exam.

I pushed myself up to stand and walked over to the door to open it slightly so I could hear if Oscar was coming down the hall.

"Martha, did you give Dr. Sebastian the letter from the Sydney Institute?" I heard the receptionist ask the nurse, Martha Perkins.

I really liked Martha. She was an older woman who seemed to understand the mothering touch I was so craving lately. Instantly, I knew that was my current issue because Little One started to bounce around.

It was like we were already bonded or somehow in sync with our intuitions. This was a little secret I had kept from Oscar. I didn't want him to feel left out of the bonding with Little One. It would hurt his feelings.

"I left it on his desk," Martha responded to receptionist. "Don't worry. I might not agree with the letter, but it's what he wants to do. So you can stop policing me now. I've been here much longer than you."

I started to follow the usual instructions to get ready for the exam as I kept a close ear to the door.

Martha's tone was much different from how I'd ever heard it. There was a bit that was almost threatening to the receptionist, but we all had a job to do, and I'd known Martha to be on top of everything as my nurse.

"There you are." Oscar hurried into the room, almost out of breath, and shut the door behind him. "What? Is something wrong? Did I miss the doctor?"

"No. I was sorta eavesdropping on a conversation that had nothing to do with me." I wondered what it was about but quickly forgot it once Dr. Sebastian walked in.

I wrapped the piece of thin tissue blanket around me and sat down on the exam table.

"Good morning, June." He had his eyes dead set on me and walked with confidence across the room with his arm extended for a handshake. "You are looking mighty good."

He had well-kept salt-and-pepper hair, a tidy mustache, and bright-white teeth to go with his tan complexion.

"In fact, I think you look just like Darla when she was along the same time as you." The big smile never left his face. "You know, she was one of my first patients out of medical school." He then turned to shake Oscar's hand and greet him.

"I do know you were the one who delivered me." I didn't go into detail about how I knew only because Darla had left behind a journal and that was how I had found him. I'd really wanted to know why Darla hadn't used a spiritualist doctor but had never read or found it in her journal.

Somehow, going to the same doctor made me feel like Darla was around me. When I'd first learned I was a spiritualist, I could feel her and my father's presence. I'd even seen them twice since I'd found my gift.

But I'd felt nothing since I'd been pregnant, and I honestly thought I'd feel them more.

"Uh-oh, where did the happy face go?" Dr. Sebastian asked me as he hit the doorbell-looking button on the wall, which singled the nurse to come in so we could start my exam.

"She seems to be doing that a lot lately." Oscar had stepped into the conversation, which I didn't like.

Instead of biting Oscar's head off, I took a few deep breaths and calmly tried to tell Dr. Sebastian everything I was feeling.

"Sometimes Little One isn't moving around as much or not at all." I lay back on the table as the nurse had suggested I do and put my feet up in those stirrups. "I can't help but wonder if everything is okay."

"I told June that there wasn't much space to move around in there." Oscar was doctoring the doctor while the doctor examined me.

Dr. Sebastian gave me a look like he understood what I was going through with Oscar, and in my gut, I knew he was telling me how all soon-to-be fathers acted this way. His gentle smile assured me it was normal soon-to-be-father banter.

"Still, if June has a concern, then we should check it out." Dr. Sebastian's response put my intuition into overdrive, making me crave a Ding Dong.

He pushed on my belly, and nothing. Little One didn't budge.

Dr. Sebastian grabbed the ultrasound machine while the nurse rubbed the gel over my belly.

"I think we'll just get a few pictures today. Help put everyone at ease." Dr. Sebastian had a confident smile on his face, but the depth of his eyes held some concern that only I could see.

I rested silently on the table with my head turned to see the monitor as the doctor rolled the ultrasound wand all over my belly.

"Look at Little One," Oscar broke the uncomfortable silence in the room, "in frog position."

"That's different." Dr. Sebastian noticed it too. "I've never seen a baby in this position before." He flipped off the monitor after he pushed a few buttons on the keyboard, printing out the ultrasound.

The nurse wiped off my belly, and Dr. Sebastian put his hand out to help me sit up.

"June, the baby's heartbeat is good. Strong. But I think you're right about the movement." He slid a glance at Oscar. "I think you're right too. It's tight quarters in there but still enough room for some movement. So what I'm going to do is have you come back in tomorrow morning for a scheduled ultrasound with movement."

"What is that?" I asked, putting my hand out for Oscar to not ask any questions when I noticed his mouth had flung open.

"It's an ultrasound that we strap around the belly. You'll be here for a couple of hours so we can monitor how many times the baby moves along with the heart rate. It'll actually give us a good baseline on when we expect the baby will make an appearance into the world on its own or if we have to help a little."

"Help?" Oscar blurted.

"You know, inducing labor is something we look at if June or the baby seems to be in any stress. Which would be fine if we had to induce, since the baby is already well-developed." The doctor gave me a much-needed reassuring smile. "You're far enough along to where if you had the baby, everyone would be fine."

I started to tear up. Oscar rushed over to my side. Dr. Sebastian and the nurse left. I could hear them talking behind the closed door, but it was too muffled to make out what they were saying.

"You're going to be fine. Little One is going to be fine." Oscar tried to say all the right words to make me feel better, but it didn't help.

CHAPTER THREE

"You're not worried, are you?" Oscar asked as soon as he got me into the car.

"I guess my silence gave it away." I continued to knead on my belly to get Little One to move, but there was nothing.

"Like the doctor said, everything is probably fine, but you can have the baby anytime." He reached over and took my hand. "Look at me."

There was no hiding the tears along my lids that clouded his face when I looked over.

"Honey." He slid across the bench seat and curled his arms around me, nestling my head into his neck. He stroked my hair. "Little One is going to be fine. What if the baby is as stubborn as you and me? Tired of getting poked and prodded? Has a great intuition like someone else I know and knew there was a doctor's visit?" His words did put a smile on my face. "I don't know a single kid or person who really enjoys going to the doctor. Do you?"

"You're right." I pushed back and wiped the tears from my cheeks. "I guess I could be like Sylvia and have lost seven babies."

"Sylvia?" Oscar asked and scooted back across the seat so we could get out of there.

"She's one of Dr. Sebastian's patients who has been going through

IVF." I told Oscar about the conversation I'd had with her and how she'd put on a brave face through it all.

"Amazing." Oscar shook his head and turned into one of the malls in Locust Grove. "We are lucky."

"Yes, we are, and I forgot that until we got into the car. I know how I feel right now, thinking my fully developed baby is in danger when all Sylvia wants is to be pregnant." My struggles seemed so trivial, but they were my struggles and diminished no less. "Where are we going?"

"I thought we'd stop by Baby Forever and check out the baby furniture." Oscar was always full of surprises. "They have different baby things from Potions, Wands, and Beyond. You might like something here that we can take home today."

"Oscar!" I let out a cry, and the tears started all over again.

"If I'd known I was going to make you cry, I wouldn't've brought you here. It's supposed to make you happy." He had a confused look on his face.

"You do make me happy. These are happy tears." I laughed, knowing he was unable to figure out my mood, which I couldn't figure out, either, and didn't expect him to. "Let's go."

He parked in one of the designated expecting-mothers spots in the parking lot.

"Do you think we can get you one of those fake pregnant bellies so that when we aren't pregnant anymore, we can still score one of these spots?" he joked, but it was a great idea.

"*We* aren't pregnant?" I questioned the "we."

"Yeah. I'm also having a need for some ice cream after we leave too." He winked and helped me out of the car.

Baby Forever was one of the national box stores that carried everything you could possibly want for a child. Of course, they had many more options than our little Potions, Wands, and Beyond. The real difference between the two, which made Oscar and me question items, was the fact that the items for Little One at Potions, Wands, and Beyond were blessed and smudged, and carried protection for the Little One.

The merchandise at Baby Forever was simply made, shipped, and bought without a care in the world. That included evil, and we didn't need any evil drama in our life.

"Oscar." I gasped and hurried over to the display cribs when I noticed one with a star and a moon. I had my hands rested on my belly. "It's not exact, but it is similar."

Little One kicked, knocking my charm bracelet around my wrist and making it jingle.

Oscar's face had shock written on it, as he, too, had seen and heard the bracelet.

"It looks like Little One approves." He put both hands on each side of my belly and bent down. "You are so loved." He gently kissed my belly.

"Ahh." There was a chuckle behind us. "First-time parents?"

We turned around and noticed an employee of Baby Forever had been watching our intimate moment.

"I guess you can tell." I laughed.

"The moms always act like this with each pregnancy, but the dads get pretty emotional about the first one." He put his hand out to shake Oscar's. "Congrats, man."

"Thank you." Oscar was so full of pride. I'd not seen him like this since the day he'd graduated from the police academy. "We are a little excited to find a crib with this mobile."

"Perfect choice," the employee agreed. "Do we know what we are having? Boy? Girl?"

"No." I shook my head and played with my charm bracelet. "We are going to wait to find out."

While the man started to tell various stories about customers and the quality of the items, my mind wandered to when Little One had kicked my charm bracelet. I never took off my bracelet. In fact, it was filled with charms given to me by my fairy god cat, Mr. Prince Charming.

For some reason, it was Mr. Prince Charming's spiritual duty to keep me safe or warn me from danger by giving me a charm.

I knew when he dropped a charm at my feet, I had to be extra cautious, and when Little One kicked my charm bracelet—not my arm, my hand, or my fingers but my charm bracelet—my intuition rang out within my soul like a gong.

It was one of those things between Little One and me that I would keep from Oscar. There were visible signs of stress on Oscar's face from what the doctor had said and the upcoming testing tomorrow that there was no more need to worry him than I needed to.

Besides, I didn't even understand it enough to know if Little One knew something or not. It was my spiritual gift that had me on edge.

"Do you want the furniture?" Oscar asked me, his eyes searching to see where my mind had wandered off to.

"I do think it's lovely." I looked at the white furniture the mobile came with and smiled when I read the poem etched on the end of the bed. "You are my sun, my moon, and all my stars." I laughed out loud at the E.E. Cummings quote.

"Are you okay?" Oscar smiled. Gently, he put a hand on my stomach to see if it was Little One making me giggle.

"Can you excuse us for a minute?" I asked the employee.

When he was safely out of ear's reach, I told Oscar, "It's perfect. My dad used to read poetry to Darla." I recalled the memory, which must've been buried deep in my mind. "I can remember him reading that to her. I think it's a sign."

"June." Oscar was so emotional. He curled me back into his arms. He whispered, "Darla and Otto are really reaching out to you. This is a sign that everything is going to be fine."

Oscar's words put a bolt of electricity in my body. There was something not fine. It wasn't about Little One. It was something else, something I couldn't put a finger on, but I knew to keep alert.

When the employee came back, I told him, "We will take it," as I played with the various charms dangling from my bracelet. "Is it in stock?"

"I'll go check." There was excitement in his voice. "Do you have a truck?"

"We will make it work." Oscar was good at making things work with a touch of his wand, which made me tingly to watch.

There was nothing like seeing Oscar use his spiritual gift, especially when he used the wand.

With the purchase in the back of the El Camino and me belted in the seat, Oscar put the car in drive and sped back to Whispering Falls, where we were greeted by our friends, who had magically known we'd gotten the furniture.

They all stood outside of their shops to wave as we drove down the main street and up the hill to our little cottage that overlooked Whispering Falls. It had the best views in town and had belonged to my parents.

"Do you think we should be looking into buying a bigger house?" Oscar asked me once we were parked.

"I don't think so. My parents had me here." I wondered why Oscar would ask such a thing. "I don't foresee us growing out of it just yet."

I got out of the car and met Mr. Prince Charming at the door.

"Hey, buddy." I rubbed him on his head as he did his signature figure eights around my ankles.

He stopped after I'd opened the door, darted in the little family room, and jumped on the back of one of the couches.

The little cottage was a cozy home. The natural wood walls accented the vibrant-orange fabric on the chairs and couches, which created all the comfort we needed. The layout was a family room and kitchen in one and a hallway with a bedroom off to the left and a bathroom across it on the right.

Oscar and I both knew it was a little tight, but the baby would only need a little room, so Oscar and Colton Lance, the other wizard and officer with the Whispering Falls Police, had been framing a small addition to the cottage that was almost finished.

"So glad Colton got the finishing touches on the room done this morning." Oscar came into the house. "We can just start setting up the furniture now."

I eyeballed him, knowing the room had been nowhere near finished when I'd left for work that morning.

Oscar didn't dare give me eye contact, so I knew he'd used his magic or had Colton use his to get the room ready. After I heard some rustling of the grass outside and looked out the kitchen window and saw Colton coming up the hill, it confirmed that Oscar had had Colton come up and do a little wand waving.

"Did you see it?" Oscar asked me.

"Did you?" I questioned to let him know I knew exactly what he was up to. "We will talk about this later."

There was a warning tone to my voice because we'd agreed we would use as little magic as possible when it came to Little One. Oscar and I had both been raised with zero magic. We were able to function in the mortal world and the magical world, which none of our spiritual friends were capable of doing.

We wanted that for Little One, or I thought we'd agreed on that, including building the extra room. Apparently, he'd not been so up front with Colton, because by the time I walked back outside to the car then came back and put my purse on the kitchen counter, Oscar had already gotten all the boxes out of the car, and the furniture had been magically all set up in the newly finished baby room with stars and moons galore.

"Too much?" Colton asked when he must've noticed the shock on my face. "We can take off a few stars and moons."

The entire ceiling of the room looked as though it were covered with real stars and moons. The deep-blue backdrop had varying sizes of twinkling stars, and the moons were strategically placed as the lighting for the room.

"The moons have a dimmer switch too." Colton didn't bother using his hand to control them. He flicked the wand in this hand to do all the work.

I tried to say something to Colton about how Oscar and I didn't want to use magic for Little One, but his big brown puppy dog eyes and messy blond hair made him look as excited about the baby's arrival as Oscar was.

"Knock, knock." I heard the familiar voice coming from the front of my cottage. "I've brought some treats."

"Ophelia!" I was delighted to know it was her before I'd seen her. I hurried up the hall, where I found my dear friend, a pretty young woman with long red hair, standing next to Mr. Prince Charming. "Ophelia Biblio, are you giving him chocolate?"

"Why, yes, I am." She grinned from ear to ear, knowing a mortal cat couldn't eat any sort of chocolate, but a fairy god cat was an entirely different creature. "And I'm going to give you some too."

"Hi, dear friend. Your partner and my spouse have really used a lot of magic today." I shook my head and took a June's Gem from the Wicked Good Bakery box she'd set on the table. "I need to sit." I eased down onto one of the kitchen table chairs and slumped my shoulders as I took a bite, and the stress melted away.

"You look stressed. I'm sorry." She came over and sat down in the chair next to me. "I tried to tell Colton that you wanted Little One to be part spiritual and part mortal, but he said Oscar needed the room done now."

"So much for bicoastal." I let the idea go as I enjoyed every single morsel of the tasty treat Raven Mortimer had lovingly named after me and created due to my obsession with the Ding Dong. "You are going to love the baby's furniture. The boys are wanding it together as we eat."

"Oh, June." Ophelia giggled and slipped a book from her satchel. "You have a wicked sense of humor that I hope Little One inherits." She slid the book across the table. "I ordered this book for you. It was written by a spiritualist baby doctor, and since I know you are using a mortal doctor, I figured you could just read up on things that might seem out of the ordinary for you."

I looked at the book.

"The doctor is from our village out west." Ophelia and Colton had moved to our village from across the country, and she'd opened Ever

After Books, and he became the police officer, making the village council come to a new age with new rules.

The number-one rule in the bylaws stated that spiritualists couldn't read other spiritualists without their permission. That meant that I couldn't use my intuition to tap into what Ophelia was feeling, and she couldn't use her abilities as a witch to read me.

Though it was a rule, I couldn't deny there were a few ways around this.

Rule number two was that you must live in Whispering Falls to own a shop here. This, along with the fact that Darla wasn't a spiritualist, was why she couldn't keep A Dose of Darla open, which had been located where my shop was today.

Bylaw three stated that there could be only one shop per spiritual family, and that included if you were dating, living with, or married to a spiritualist. One shop—which Darla was exempt from because she wasn't a spiritualist.

That bylaw had quickly changed after Oscar and I had decided to get married, and for the greater good of the spiritual community, it was better for us to be here and love our community as we provided our gifts. In the case of Colton and Ophelia, they'd originally kept their relationship on the down-low, but all was good. Now, if a spiritual family moved in and would like to open two shops, a proposal was sent to the village council and was voted upon with the greater good of the community in the heart of the decision.

Rule number four was actually about committing or being accused of committing a crime. You couldn't be arrested until it had been proven, but you also couldn't leave the village until the crime was solved.

"I'm not sure what you need to know, other than the fact that when Little One has a glowing bowel movement, apparently it means they need to be smudged with something." Ophelia's body trembled as though the thought of baby poop meant something. "I don't know. I guess if you saw glowing poo, you'd look it up, but I figured I'd give you a leg up on it."

"Thank you." I couldn't help but be filled with gratitude, as my friends in the village had accepted my way of bringing up Little One. "It's going to be difficult trying to teach both worlds."

"I'm not going to tell you I think it's going to be easy, but I will tell you that I believe you'll find the perfect solution." She drew her hand up and down, a little gold sparkle tailing her gesture. "Look at you. You're a perfect example."

"Speaking of being perfect people." I eyed her, wanting to take the conversation off of me for a moment. "When are you two going to have a baby?"

"It just so happens we are going to go for a romantic getaway for a couple of nights tomorrow since Colton is off the next few days." She looked so happy.

"Oh." I rubbed my hands together vigorously in hopes they'd return with a new one on the way.

"I almost forgot." Her eyes widened. "How did the doctor's appointment go? Any birthing dates?"

"I'm a little worried, actually." I leaned in and spoke in a low voice so Oscar couldn't hear me. "The baby isn't moving as much, and the doctor confirmed there was still some room in there to move about, so they are going to have me come back in the morning for some tests. But he did say. . ." I wanted to be clear that everything looked fine, because Ophelia was giving me that look that was a cross between empathy, shock, and not knowing what to say or think. "The baby was growing healthily, and all Little One's vitals were perfect."

"Oh good." She lifted her hands to her mouth in a prayer position, looking up. "Any idea on boy or girl?"

"Nope. I refuse to know." It was kind of fun not knowing what Little One was going to be. No matter what, the baby was going to be loved beyond measure. The gender didn't matter to us.

"That doesn't help with the baby shower, which I'm sure you heard about in the newspaper this morning." She and a couple of my other close spiritualist friends along with one of my mortal friends, Adeline, who knew about our little secret, were throwing me the shower at the gathering rock. "You know Bella. She's all about the glitz and glamor. If she could pull the stars and moon down for you with pink sparkles for the shower, she would."

Mr. Prince Charming jumped off the back of the couch and trotted over. He circled around my legs before he jumped up on his hind legs, batting at my charm bracelet.

"He loves to play," Ophelia said in delight just as he spit something on the floor.

My heart sank. Mr. Prince Charming never played. The only time he batted at my bracelet was when he was trying to tell me I needed to have protection for something.

"What on earth?" Ophelia drew back in disgust, just like she'd done with the thought of glowing baby poo. Her nose curled, and her lips contorted.

"Speaking of Bella." I picked up the silver elephant charm and knew Mr. Prince Charming had a message for me.

But what?

CHAPTER FOUR

Bella's Baubles was like all the other stores in Whispering Falls—a quaint cream cottage with a pink wood door that was adorned with different-colored jewels. The sun hit each jewel just right, showing its brilliant color.

The pinks played up the blues today, making me wonder if the spirit world was trying to tell me something about Little One.

Mr. Prince Charming darted right on inside after I'd opened the heavy door into the small entryway that led to two other doors. One of them had a mailbox on it, and the other had Bella's sign on it that read her shop hours, Morning to Night.

Every time I read the sign, I couldn't stop myself from smiling. Bella Van Lou always had a sunny disposition that brightened anyone's day, which was perfect for her spiritual gift of Astrology.

Her shop was the gorgeous jewelry store where Mr. Prince Charming seemed to snag those charms I needed for my bracelet.

Bella looked up from behind one of the jewelry display counters with a loupe up to her right eye.

"June and Little One." Bella's cheeks rounded with her grin, exposing the small gap between her two front teeth. Her long blond hair framed her face and cascaded down her small body. "I've been waiting patiently to see you."

She put the loupe down. Mr. Prince Charming had jumped on top of the counter to greet her, as he always did.

"You are a very good fairy god cat." She patted him and showered him with compliments.

The heels of her pointy boots clicked as her five-foot-two body came around to give me a hug but not before she rubbed Little One. "I bet you get tired of us doing that."

"It's fine." I *was* tired of everyone doing that. "But I read in Darla's journal how everyone here touched her belly, and when she asked Eloise about it, Eloise told her about the good fortune bestowed upon the baby with the silent offerings with the touches."

"That's right." Bella went on to further explain, "Every one of us is giving Little One a special blessing to enter this world safely, because you do know evil lurks, which is why I'm sure you are here." She reached down and opened the palm of my hand, where the elephant charm was resting. With ease, she unclasped my charm bracelet and took it behind the counter.

Mr. Prince Charming sat next to Bella as if he were making sure the work was done properly as she put the small elephant charm on the bracelet.

"The elephant is a magnificent choice," she said to Mr. Prince Charming. His tail slowly wagged across the glass display case. "God of luck, fortune, and protection and is a blessing upon all new projects. And you, June, dear, have a lot of new projects going."

"Yes, I do." I wondered why, if it was such good luck, he had given it to me. "Wait, you said protection? Does this have to do with the baby?"

Bella sucked in a deep breath.

"Mewl, meeewwwl," Mr. Prince Charming cried out.

"It is about keeping you and Little One safe at your doctor appointments. Keeping your intuition intact so you'll make informed decisions, though I am not reading you." She made it clear she wasn't going against the bylaws, because that would summon the Order of Elders, and I had no time to entertain the three Marys.

Mary Lynn, Mary Ellen, and Mary Sue were the three that made up the elders. They were what I'd call the judges and jury of the spiritual world, and that included all the villages from the west to the east and from the north down to the south.

Most of the time, they did more harm than good, so anything to keep myself or the entire village safe, I was going to do.

CHAPTER FIVE

"*E*verything *is okay, Little One.*" *I tried to calm the crying baby by bouncing it close to my chest.* "*Everything is okay,*" *I assured the baby and pulled it down to get a look at the sweet little face. My eyes squinted to see through the darkness of the dimly light space.* "*I know you're hungry. Food will be here soon.*"

The nightmare knocked me awake, and I found myself sitting straight up in bed. The shower was on, and the bathroom light was lit. I reached over to Oscar and felt the empty spot in the bed.

I moved my gaze to the side table and tapped Madame Torres.

"What is it you wish to seek? And it had better be good at this hour." Her grumpy voice came through the ball, but her face didn't. I was positive she hadn't had time to get her makeup on, and an appearance at seven a.m. was not high on her priority list.

"I had a nightmare." I tried to swallow, but my mouth was so dry that my voice cracked. "Did you see?"

"I am seeing only my eyelids." She wasn't being very cooperative. "And that is all I've been seeing."

"It was me trying to feed a crying baby. I couldn't see through the dark." I'd not had a nightmare in a long time. "You know when I have a nightmare, it has some sort of meaning, in case you needed a reminder."

My familiars, Madame Torres and Mr. Prince Charming, had it pretty good. I didn't require much of them like the other spiritualists did of their familiars, so waking her up once in the past year didn't seem to be an unreasonable request.

"There is nothing in the future to be held. The food source for the Little One will be provided by your own body, and there will be plenty for the Little One." Her words were as smooth as the lines waving within her globe of serene orange. "Go back to bed. Little One needs rest."

Her ball went black.

Little One wasn't moving. I placed my hand on my belly and pushed a few times in various places like the doctor had, but nothing happened.

"Mr. Prince Charming?" I called and used my foot to feel down at the bottom of the bed, where he'd moved now that my belly had taken up his spot, and Little One loved to kick him, which gave my fairy god cat little sleep.

My foot turned up an empty space.

"June, are you okay?" Oscar walked into the room, using a towel to dry his wet hair. I'd not heard the shower turn off.

"I had a nightmare."

My words put an uneasy look on his face. He came around to my side of the bed and sat down. He placed his hand on my stomach.

"A nightmare, nightmare?" He was asking if it was like the other nightmares I'd had that warned me something awful was going to happen.

"It didn't make me feel good." I didn't want to commit to the fact that it was like the others. I was already worried and didn't need Oscar to worry, but the idea that I was going to run out of food for the Little One frightened me to the depths of my core. "I was unable to feed baby."

All the particulars of the nightmare didn't matter. The important factor was the inability to provide food, and no parent wanted that.

"Do you think my body is not nourishing Little One, and that's the problem?" I questioned him.

"The only way to find out is the tests this morning." He ran his thumb along my face. "I don't like to see so much worry on your face. It's not good for you or the baby."

"I know. I'm probably worrying over nothing, but I'd like to know if the nutrition isn't going through my unbiblical cord." My mind rolled back through the meals I'd eaten over the last couple of days and zeroed in on all the Ding Dongs I'd eaten. "Maybe it's the sweets."

"Maybe you should have one a day instead of. . ." He winked. "Ten."

"You joke about ten, but I probably did eat ten yesterday." I felt a little better with some sort of explanation that I'd had the nightmare due to eating too much sugar, and my intuition was telling me through the nightmare to cut back on the sweets because it wasn't good for Little One. "Just to be sure, I'll ask the doctor."

"I'll call off work and let Colton handle it," Oscar said.

"No!" I pushed the covers off of my legs and sat on the edge of the bed next to Oscar. "He's taking Ophelia on a romantic getaway, so you have to work. I can go to the doctor by myself. I'll be just fine."

"Are you sure?" he asked. "Because I can get someone to look after the department."

That was the thing with the spiritual world. If Oscar did have an emergency, he could get one of us to look after the shop, and we could easily get in touch with him if we needed to.

"I'm positive. I think I'll get up and get ready because I'd like to stop by the Piggly Wiggly to see Adeline and check on the product line."

"Good idea." He gave me a kiss on the head and got up to go get his Whispering Falls Police uniform on. He tucked his wand securely in the utility belt. "It might do you some good to get in some mortal girl time and do a little business to take your mind off things. Is Faith at A Charming Cure?"

"She is." I pushed up to stand.

Mr. Prince Charming darted out from underneath the bed and rubbed against me before he jumped up on the nightstand, knocking into Madame Torres.

Her globe lit up fire red, and her eyes widened, showing the whites all dotted with red squiggly lines, like she'd had a rough night.

"If you dare knock me off this table again, I will curse you, bringing bad things upon you," she warned Mr. Prince Charming, only instigating him to take a big swipe at her with his paw.

I grabbed her before he could knock her to the ground like he'd done before.

"You two, stop it. I don't need this stress," I warned both of them. "We will have a calm household for Little One. Do you two understand?"

I looked between them for one of them to go first, but with their stubbornness, I knew it was going to take me to encourage it.

"On the count of three, you'll both agree. One, two, three."

I took a deep breath as Mr. Prince Charming wagged his tail high in the air and Madame Torres responded with, "Fine."

"Good. I'm going to take you with me today since Oscar can't go and I'm needing someone to talk to," I told Madame Torres, which got an eyebrow twitch response.

"You're not going to put me into that bag, are you?" She was awful at taking any sort of directions, and I'd never seen a familiar not take orders as she did.

"Why did I get a sassy crystal ball?" I asked Oscar after I waddled down the hall.

He'd prepared me my only cup of coffee for the day.

"Because you can handle anything." He sat my coffee on the table and pulled out my chair. "You promise me you'll call me as soon as your test is finished?"

"I will, and I plan on coming back after that, so I'll go see Adeline first." I gave him a kiss on his lips when he bent down. "Have a wonderful day. I love you."

"I love you." He ran his hand down my head. Then he put his hand on my stomach and bent down. "I love you, Little One." He kissed my belly, and off he went.

Mr. Prince Charming was too busy cleaning himself to worry about

Madame Torres and me. I'd set her on the table and decided to look through a few more pages of Darla's journal while I savored the coffee.

Today, Little One, as Otto loves to call the baby, has been very active. Dr. Sebastian said he was pleased with the baby's progress. Otto would die if he knew Eloise had me drink some crazy concoction to find out what sex the baby is.

A girl. My very own girl.

Eloise said her brother is having a baby boy. We thought it would be fun to have them play together, but he'd be a dark sider like Eloise, and I'm not sure Otto would go for that. Even though Otto doesn't see all the differences between the good siders and dark siders, he knows they're there, and it's the rule. This is our biggest fight and the difference between the mortal world versus his spiritual world.

I think there need to be changes in the rules, and I can only hope my sweet baby girl will have some mortal genes and spiritual genes so she can be the one to make a change in the spiritual world. I feel it. I feel this girl is special. She's going to do amazing things with her life.

I can't wait to see those in her as she grows. I can only pray for the day I see her greatness. I can feel it. Only... Eloise warned me of my fate.

I ran my hand across her words, wondering how she knew I would be able to make her wishes come true. I had made several changes to the bylaws of the spiritual world since I'd been blessed to know my gift, but how did she feel it?

I ran my hand all over my stomach as I closed my eyes to tap into any sort of intuition about Little One. I was getting nothing.

"I'm so worried." I tapped Madame Torres. "What if the baby has Darla's genes? I know things can skip a generation."

"You will know, as the council sought you out. As Little One grows, you'll see. Learn. Teach." Madame Torres's voice had a little reassurance in it.

Instead of dwelling on it, I knew the answers were only going to come through Dr. Sebastian, and that meant I had to get myself up and get ready.

Long gone were my skinny jeans and little black dresses, but I was able to wear a cute pair of maternity leggings with a short-sleeved shirt and a pair of tennis shoes. If I was going to lie there while Little One was being monitored, I wasn't going to get all fancied up like I had for the every-other-week doctor appointments.

Getting behind the wheel of the 1988 El Camino felt good. Mr. Prince Charming had decided he wasn't staying behind after he watched me put Madame Torres into the bag, and she grumbled and mumbled the entire time.

He took his usual spot on the dashboard, where he curled up so the sun warmed him as it shone through the windshield.

The Piggly Wiggly was a grocery store franchise in Locust Grove that my friend Adeline owned. I'd met her many years ago when she'd come into A Charming Cure. With my half-mortal and half-spiritualist personality, I was able to have a friendship with her. She was smart and could see through anything I was doing that wasn't mortal. Eventually, I did end up letting her in on the secret of Whispering Falls and how I fit in.

Having my products in her store was my first step into the big box stores, where mortals could find a lot of my products.

There wasn't a parking spot in the Piggly Wiggly parking lot for expectant mothers, and I made a mental note to get on Adeline about that, in a teasing way, of course, and I parked in the closest spot I could find.

Mr. Prince Charming wasn't a therapy dog or cat, so technically, he wasn't allowed in the grocery store, but somehow through his magical gifts, he was able to go in with me and stay out of the customers' sight.

"Do not touch," I told myself when I walked past the bakery and saw the display case filled with some of June's Gems along with various other sweet treats from Wicked Good Bakery.

Just the fact that Adeline had contracted with Raven Mortimer to sell Raven's products showed how amazing Adeline was.

It was a pleasant surprise to see how many of the bottles for the A Charming Cure end cap display were gone.

I looked around and carefully listened to pick the right moment to snap my fingers to refill the display with the most spectacular bottles so no one would notice.

"Lovely." I made sure I touched each bottle.

The bottles were very pleasing to the eyes, which made the product noticeable, but the contents of the bottles were what brought all the customers back. In situations like these stores, where I couldn't read the customer and make the exact potion for the bottle they needed, I had come up with a system for the bottles.

I was able to create these bottles so that when they were touched by the right customer, the contents were able to mature into the right potion for what ailed the recipient. It was a very creative concept I'd come up with after I'd made the national deal with Head-to-Toes Works.

To that day, my products flew off the shelves of all the stores nationwide.

"You might be in charge one day." I patted my belly and stood back to take in the gorgeous display.

"June." Adeline's voice put a smile on my face before I even looked at her. "I didn't know you were coming by."

"I didn't either."

We hugged, and she looked down at my stomach with that amazing and warm smile she always had on her face.

"Big. I know."

"Do you have a doctor's appointment?" she asked only because she knew I rarely left Whispering Falls these days.

"I do at nine." I had very little time to chat with her, as the morning was getting away from me. "And it's going to be a long one."

She invited me to talk to her back in their employee room, where I quickly gave her a synopsis of what had happened at the doctor's appointment yesterday as well as what I'd read in Darla's journal. She'd always been such a great listener and supportive. I'd never forget her being there for me when Oscar and I had broken up and he'd gone on a few dates. It tore me up inside.

She was an amazing friend that I was ever so grateful for.

"And what does your intuition say?" she asked.

"It doesn't say anything." I sighed, my shoulders slumped. Mr. Prince Charming was sitting on the table, watching us. "He's not left my side."

"Of course he hasn't."

She leaned over to pat him, and he batted at her swinging strand of sandy blond hair. Both of us laughed.

"He might be your familiar, but at the end of the day, he's still a cat."

"You have that right." I watched as two of my best friends played around. "I also wanted to thank you for co-hosting the baby shower. I know it's not easy being a mortal among a lot of headstrong spiritualists."

"You know, the secret I've found is to keep my mouth shut and let them do the planning. I'm bringing the food, and the rest of it is up to them. If there is one thing we different worlds have in common, it's eating. I've got that covered."

Someone on the loudspeaker called her to come to the customer service desk.

"I've got to go."

"Me too." I was already going to be cutting it close getting to my appointment, and I couldn't help but think it was my way of procrastinating for the test. "I'll walk up front with you."

We said our goodbyes, and before I knew it, Mr. Prince Charming and I were looking at the glaring lights on top of at least five deputy sheriffs' cars parked all around the doctor's office building.

"What is going on?" I questioned and parked across the street to watch and decide whether I should try to go in or call.

Out of the corner of my eye, I saw my bag glowing. It was one way Madame Torres used to get my attention.

Mr. Prince Charming had his paws up on the passenger door, staring out the window at the situation. He was doing his own assessment.

I reached down into my bag and pulled out the glowing globe. Madame Torres was swirling pixelated images among the wave of purple and black.

"Madame Torres, what do you see?" I instructed her to show me.

The pixelation joined the purple and black swirls, making them all one big blur before the globe became a gray-and-white screen like a television.

"There is danger lurking around you," she warned. I held her closer to my eyes to get a good look at what she was showing me. "This is not a good place for you or the Little One. Thou must leave. Thou must turn around and go home to the safety of Whispering Falls."

"Ouch!" I gasped and dropped the ball onto the seat, grabbing my wrist. "I think it electrocuted me."

"What are you doing?" Madame Torres burst out in anger. "Do not drop me!" Her eyes glowed yellow, the lids painted in blues and whites, and her lips were shaded a blood red. Her face bounced around the globe in the fluid, replacing the video she was playing.

Mr. Prince Charming jumped from the passenger side to on top of my stomach to get a look at the charm bracelet.

"I feel like my bracelet electrocuted me." I looked up at Mr. Prince Charming as he tried to stay balanced on my belly as Little One came to life. "What on earth?" My focus went from the bracelet to the baby.

"June." The knock on the driver's-side window caused me to jump.

"Martha." I put my hand to my chest, relieved it was her. "You scared me. What is going on?"

"Roma is dead." Her eyes filled with tears. "I'm not sure what happened to her, but the cleaning crew comes every morning before we open, and when they were throwing the trash away, they found her body in there. Shot."

Martha's face was filled with sorrow.

"Shot? As in murdered?" The words left my mouth, and my intuition went on high alert. My hand immediately went to my bracelet.

"Can I please sit down in your car? The heat is already scorching, and the sheriff won't let me leave until I give some sort of statement." She blinked, releasing the tears that were dammed up in her eyes.

"Of course." I leaned over to unlock the passenger door, which was hard for me these days.

Mr. Prince Charming jumped up on the dash. He sat straight up with his eyes on Martha.

"This feels so good." She adjusted the air vent on her side and jerked back when she finally noticed the white cat. "Oh."

"I hope you're not allergic to cats. He's my helper cat." I shrugged because I couldn't tell her he was my familiar fairy god cat without sounding like a lunatic.

"That explains why the baby isn't moving." She went to put her hand on me, and I was going to ask her what she meant, but she ended up picking up Madame Torres. "Snow globe. I haven't seen one of these things in years." She shook it, and when nothing happened, she shook it harder.

"Yes, a snow globe with lots of glitter." I said it loud enough that Madame Torres could hear me and do something.

I gulped and watched the silver glitter fall around the globe, knowing Madame Torres was probably feeling the effects of being seasick. She didn't do well with being shaken.

"I'm sorry. This is very sentimental to me. It belonged to an ancestor, and I brought it with me to soothe me while I had the test." I took Madame Torres and put her on the dashboard next to Mr. Prince Charming.

He was sly. He batted at the globe, knowing I wouldn't get on him and Madame Torres couldn't be heard with a mortal around.

"No, no." I nervously laughed to get him to stop tormenting Madame Torres. When he looked at me, I could have sworn there was some pleasure on his feline face. "Leave the snow globe alone."

"Wow, it's like the cat knows what you're saying," Martha noted when Mr. Prince Charming went back to staring at her. "Back to the baby. You must have high anxiety to have a therapy cat, which is why the baby probably isn't moving."

I let Martha ramble on about stress and how the baby could feel it, but I knew better. I also continued to let her believe Mr. Prince Charming was a therapy cat when I never said he was.

Her behavior was odd after she'd just found out her coworker had been murdered, which made me want to question her more.

"Do they know who shot Roma?" I asked and watched over her shoulder as the deputies continued to gather and talk in front of the office.

"No. And there's no video. Dr. Sebastian is old, and he never bought into getting a security system. But I wouldn't doubt it if it was her boyfriend. She was always complaining about him and his friends. They were always encouraging her to take a stand against Dr. Sebastian's lab studies. He's from the seedy side of town."

I knew where that side of town was located. It was where I'd grown up. It was the poorer side of town. By her tone of voice, she made it sound like the criminal side of town.

Sure, it had its fair share of crime, but so did all the other areas of Locust Grove.

"Have they questioned him?" I asked her, trying to figure out what she knew.

"I have no idea. I tried to tell the officer about him, but he didn't seem to care and told me to stay put and not leave until they told me to." She brought her hand up to her mouth like she'd suddenly remembered someone had been shot. "I just can't believe it. She was a dear sweet girl. So much life ahead of her."

This was a much different attitude than I recalled Martha having yesterday when she and Roma were having a few words while I was in the exam room.

Martha continued to talk about how amazing Roma had been. Instead of concentrating on her stories, I tried to remember exactly what they had been talking about.

These days, it was hard for me to remember anything. When I'd brought that up to Dr. Sebastian at my last appointment, he told me it was normal brain activity caused by the pregnancy, bringing the term "pregnant pause" to an entirely new level.

"Oh! They are waving me over." Something flickered in her eyes and caught me off guard. "I hate to tell you that you won't be able to have your test, but they did ask me to cancel all of Dr. Sebastian's appointments. I'll call you with a reschedule day." She got out of the car and hurried back across the street, where she was met by Sheriff Sonny Butler, Oscar's friend and part-time boss.

Sonny said something to Martha and looked over at me. He waved, and I returned the gesture, signaling for him to walk over.

I left the green machine running because Mr. Prince Charming was in the car and got out to talk to Sonny.

"My goodness, you look great. Oscar sure is happy." Sonny and Oscar had gone to school together.

Sonny was the sheriff of the county where Locust Grove was located. Locust Grove had a police department within the city limits, but the county limits were the sheriff's department's job. Oscar's uncle Jordan had been the police chief of Locust Grove when we were growing up. But now Oscar was a part-time deputy with the sheriff's department when he wasn't working in Whispering Falls.

They called it double dipping, but we called it double pay.

"What on earth happened?" I asked instead of going into the fact that Oscar was going to be a wonderful father.

"The receptionist was found shot dead in the dumpster out back. As luck would have it, there's not any evidence back there so far." He shifted his eyes to my stomach. "When you due?"

"Not for a month." I rubbed my stomach. "But I was here today so Dr. Sebastian could do a test since the baby's not been moving."

"Really?" Sonny questioned, giving me closer inspection. "Let me see what I can do."

My intuition kicked in.

"Are you doing it for the safety of the baby?" I had to ask. "Or are you doing it so you can get Oscar to come help with the case?"

I knew it was the latter since Oscar was really good in the homicide department. He didn't even use his wizard skills either.

"Can't it be both?" he asked before he clicked the walkie-talkie in his hand. "Is Dr. Sebastian here yet?"

"Yes, sir. He's in his office," the deputy answered.

"I'm going to go in and see him." He motioned for me to come with him.

"I need my emotional support cat." I waddled around my car to get my bag and Mr. Prince Charming.

"So that's your cat I've heard all about." Sonny laughed and watched with a close eye as Mr. Prince Charming approached him. "I heard all about you giving Oscar fits when he and June were dating."

Mr. Prince Charming liked how Sonny addressed him personally, and I could tell because he was doing figure eights around Sonny's ankles.

"You seem like a sweet cat." Sonny reached down and ran his hand along the back of Mr. Prince Charming, sending a clump of white fur into the breeze.

"He is very sweet. Very protective." I slipped Madame Torres into my bag and locked the green machine's doors.

"Are you okay?" Sonny asked, as if he didn't have any other thing in the world to worry about.

"I'm fine." I didn't know whether Oscar had told Sonny anything about the pregnancy, but I did know Sonny had no idea we were spiritualists. "Just a test to make sure everything is going as planned."

"That's good." He held up the police tape and had me walk under it to the front door of the doctor's office.

Little One could be here quicker, especially if Dr. Sebastian felt like I needed to be induced, but Sonny didn't need to know that. "Thank you," I said when he hurried around me to grab the handle of the front door.

"Is Oscar crazy busy at the department in Whispering Falls?" Sonny's questions were starting to lead up to something.

"What exactly are you trying to ask?" I stopped in the lobby and eased myself down into the chair.

The combination of walking and stress along with Little One resting on my bladder that day had me exhausted.

"I think I'm going to need his help on this case." Sonny walked over to the door that led back to the exam rooms and disappeared.

I had just enough time to process what he meant before he and Dr. Sebastian came back through the door.

"June." Dr. Sebastian walked over with his hand extended as he normally did in the exam room. "You look very good."

"Thank you, but I think you might be a little too busy for my test." I gave him a sympathetic look because it didn't take the gift of intuition to see the stress on his face.

"No. I understand Sheriff Butcher is a good friend, and if he says I can go ahead and get you and the baby hooked up, I think we can do that." He tried to put a nice and warm smile on his face, but his eyes, which led to his soul, showed hurt and sadness. "Has the baby moved any?"

"Not a whole lot." I pushed myself up to stand. Mr. Prince Charming stayed right by my side.

"Who is this feller?" he asked.

Mr. Prince Charming stood up on his hind legs and batted at the bracelet.

"That's June and Oscar's cat, Mr. Prince Charming." Sonny chuckled. "From what Oscar tells me, he's a very protective cat with the baby."

"He's a good boy. I can see that." Dr. Sebastian gave me a sense that he had an idea about Mr. Prince Charming and who I was. "Shall we?"

Dr. Sebastian guided Mr. Prince Charming and me to the door. He turned and put his hand out when Sonny tried to come with us.

"I'm sorry. June's test is private, and we don't allow spouses or close family friends to come in. You know, she needs rest so the baby can move." He didn't wait for Sonny to protest. He closed the door to the waiting room.

Dr. Sebastian gave a slight turn of his head, as though he was trying to make sure we were following, before Mr. Prince Charming darted ahead.

"Mr. Prince Charming," I scolded the cat for thinking he could just do whatever he wanted and go anywhere he wanted. "I'm so sorry."

Dr. Sebastian went into the same room as Mr. Prince Charming and flipped on the lights. Mr. Prince Charming was already sitting on top of the reclined chair, which had a little blanket folded up neatly at the end. There was an ultrasound type of monitor next to it with a few electrical leads attached to it. He gestured for me to sit in the chair.

"June, you can have a seat and lift your shirt up. I'll get started placing these little adhesive buttons on your belly. I'll attach the electrodes to the buttons, and it'll help count how many times the baby moves." He patted my hand. "You're going to be fine. You did this with Darla, and that's how I knew to contact the Order of Elders and tell them that you could possibly be one of us."

"You..." My mouth opened then closed. I started to feel faint before everything went completely dark.

CHAPTER SIX

"Yes. Yes. I understand." I could hear Eloise Sandlewood, Oscar's aunt, talking as I was coming out of the fainting spell.

The prickly tongue on my cheek was also very familiar, and when I cracked my eyes open, Mr. Prince Charming was staring at me. He gave me a few slow blinks to let me know it was going to be okay.

"I had to say something to her. I could see in her eyes that she's been worried sick about the baby, and I had to tell her this is completely normal activity for a child of some spiritual nature about to be born. Plus..." I heard some shuffling. "I'm beside myself about Roma. If the sheriff looks too deep, I'm worried our little secret will be figured out."

"Hello?" I called when I decided that I needed to know what was going on. Even though I'd like to know how Eloise got here, I was assuming Dr. Sebastian called her somehow.

"June, thank goodness you're awake." Eloise glided into the room, her long green cloak fluttering behind her. She drew a wand from underneath the summer cloak and waved it over me. "Be the light, light worker, a light within, inspiration, awakening, soul, white witch, witch, magick, heal the world, help others, oneness, book of shadows, meditation, love, peace, safety is your grace," she chanted a few times before she brought her hands together and bowed her head toward me.

"What was that?" I asked and glanced down at my stomach, where Little One was moving around so much that the monitor I was hooked up to was going off the charts.

"There you go." She pointed at the machine when Dr. Sebastian approached. "We will go now." She pulled my shirt over my belly and smoothed it out like a tablecloth before she helped me to sit up. "The baby is just fine."

"Eloise." I took my hand back, resisting her help to get me to my feet. "I overheard you and Dr. Sebastian. He is one of us."

"Oh dear." Her brows pinched. She brought her fingertips to her short red hair and picked at the ends. "I was afraid of this."

"You're afraid of one of us finding out who I am? I'm afraid one of them is going to find out who I am." He shuffled back and forth, a little more spry than normal.

"I get it. You pretend to be all elderly, but in reality. . ." I didn't need to finish my sentence for them to nod. "It just goes to show that I'm still naive when it comes to thinking I know it all in the spiritual world." I rubbed my stomach. "So everything is really good with the baby?"

"Yes." Dr. Sebastian gave a hard nod.

"You are a real doctor."

"Yes."

"And Martha?" I asked. "Is she one of us?"

"No. She's a mortal who has worked with me for years. Normally, she's off when spiritual patients come in, or I at least keep her busy. She seems to zero in on when you are here, and so when she heard you mention the baby wasn't moving, I knew I had to order the test." In one jerk of his hand, he ripped off the receipt-looking paper the machine had spit out after Eloise did her wand waving and chanting. "This is the movement of the baby to put in your file so it appears as though you had the test."

"Sonny?" I questioned.

"No. Sonny is not. He is just your husband's friendly and nosy sheriff friend, who has been trying to come back here and check on you, but I couldn't have him see you passed out because I fear they might suspect me as the killer."

"Why would he assume such things?" I asked.

Dr. Sebastian glanced over at Eloise. She gave him a slight nod to continue.

"I was careless with some of the billing over the past few years." He paused, wrestling to find the right words.

"He has used the billing system the Order of Elders put in place for the spiritualist clients so that if he ever did get audited or someone was to come across something, the spiritual world would be covered." Eloise took the liberty of finding the words he was searching for.

"As the receptionist, Roma was in charge of filing the insurance. When I had you come in and I forgot to file the claim with the spiritual insurance…" His jaw tightened.

"So the insurance we have isn't real insurance?" I questioned.

"We always make sure that every spiritualist is covered for whatever they need. You needed an obstetrician, and since we don't have any sort of doctors in Whispering Falls, naturally, we suggested you come to Dr. Sebastian because he is one of us and is a women's and baby doctor." Eloise was talking in circles.

I'd seen her do it with others, and now she was pulling it on me.

"So you do know how to deliver babies, and you did deliver me?" I needed to be very clear.

"Oh yes. Darla was sent to me by Otto because spiritual babies can definitely be much different in the womb from mortal babies." He pointed at Little One. "And the behavior you're experiencing is the Little One growing in the last few weeks in the spiritual realm, which is a good sign that the baby won't take on mortal traits like Darla."

That put me at ease a little.

"Again, why do you think you're a suspect?" I'd accepted the fact that he was a spiritualist, and Little One was okay, and since Martha had noticed the baby not moving, he had to do the test as a cover-up to keep Dr. Sebastian's real life a secret, but I wasn't clear on why he'd be considered a suspect.

"Like Eloise said, I failed to put your insurance into the system," he started to say.

"As he's failed to do with other spiritualist insurance over the past ten years." Eloise's lashes lowered, creating a shadow on her face as the stern words echoed around the exam room. "And Roma went back into the system. She even went as far as trying to contact the insurance company and turned up nothing. After she discovered the insurance was fake, she went back into the files to see who else Dr. Sebastian had performed services on and added up the cost." Eloise pursed her lips as though she were trying to contain the anger bubbling up within. "And Roma believes he's pocketed the money."

"She's blackmailing me," he blurted. "*Was* blackmailing me. She also had a file and was pretty close to realizing exactly who we all are. She was able to identify that the various patients were from the same villages, and she put together dates of travel along with the transportation to get here."

Now he was confusing me.

"So if a patient came from the west village for a normal hysterectomy, she wondered why they wouldn't see a doctor out there instead of coming to Dr. Sebastian. All of them could've seen plenty of doctors out there. And these patients all lived in the same town, which is a spiritual town, and she traced that back." Eloise explained it much better.

I sat there speechless. One of the first things they taught you in university was how the spiritual world worked in the mortal world. It was a completely different world that was intricately meshed together. When one part of the wheel didn't work, it became the type of mess Dr. Sebastian had created that would take the whole thing down.

"So when Sonny Butcher goes to her house, he's going to find all sorts of things about us that he won't understand until he takes apart her findings?" I was trying to come up with a solution and not get so caught up in the details. "Which means we have to get to her apartment before anyone else does."

"Right." Eloise took her cloak and wrapped it around my shoulders. "And that means you and I need to go right now."

And in the blink of an eye, Eloise had used her transporting gift to make the smooth transition from the exam room to a motel room.

"She lives in a motel?" I looked around and tried to see through the darkness created by the pulled curtains.

"She and her boyfriend live here." Eloise snapped her fingers in the air. "Kids!"

The room was suddenly lit up by the fireflies she summoned from Whispering Falls. They all clung to the wall as if they were twinkling lights that'd been hung there.

"I know you are tired. I wouldn't expect anything less from you teenagers and the hours you keep, but it's time to come together for the sake of our world." She held a lot of authority, and everyone always sought her out for counsel.

The fireflies, or lightning bugs, were the teens of the spiritual world. It was very fitting, since they had all the characteristic of teenagers. They stayed up all night, ate anything they could get their little hands on, and could sleep anywhere.

It was actually very pretty around the motel room, and they lit up the place with just the right amount of light to let Eloise and me look around.

"A sheriff's deputy will be here any moment, so we need to work fast." Eloise started her search by opening drawers to shuffle through the papers.

This was one of the few times when I wish we were able to flick our noses or tug our ears like we were portrayed in the television shows. It didn't work like that. My skills were limited to my intuition and what people needed to feel good.

Eloise was actually considered multigifted, but her main job was to keep evil spirits away from Whispering Falls using her incense spiritualist talents. Every morning before dawn broke, Eloise walked down the main street in Whispering Falls with her incense burner, chanting good tidings into the smoke as it infiltrated our special town.

Locust Grove was an all-mortal community, which made it hard for us to use our gifts.

Both of us worked our way around the room, turning up nothing.

"Do you think she had some sort of private place?" Eloise questioned and took the cloak from around her shoulders. She pushed back the sides of her short hair, as it was sticking to her head from the perspiration.

"What about her car?" I questioned, thinking it was a good hiding place.

Eloise pondered the idea for a moment before the door into the motel room started to open. Light from the sun pierced the room.

Eloise snapped her fingers. The fireflies flew in a line, bombarding the skinny man who tried to enter the room like a swarm of bees.

I watched as he tried to swat left and then right, but the fireflies kept coming, creating so much chaos that the man didn't have time to notice Eloise and me as he stumbled backward, almost going over the wrought-iron railing.

Eloise grabbed her cloak and quickly flung it around both of us, transporting us back to the safety of Eloise's gazebo in her beautiful garden in the woods right behind Whispering Falls.

"Tea?" she questioned and picked up her flowered china teapot.

She filled her small teacup and held the pot over the teacup sitting in front of me on the small café table.

"And I have a variety of macarons." She snapped a tea towel off of the three-tiered dessert display in the middle of the table. The treats were a rainbow of colors. "What?"

"You don't remember what just happened?" I questioned in disbelief. "That's the thing with spiritualists." I had to get my point across. "And I can see it because I'm part mortal, but when something happens with the two worlds colliding, it's as though spiritualists let it go."

While I ranted, Eloise simply sat in her chair, eating her macarons and sipping her tea. Mr. Prince Charming appeared out of nowhere, and I continued to explain myself only because my mortal side had to be heard.

"Just like the whole thing with the boyfriend. If you were a mortal friend, we'd still be talking about it with fast-beating hearts and probably out of breath. But with you…" I gestured to her and the table scape. "You simply put it in the back of your mind and go about your day."

"June, dear…" Eloise plucked a purple macaron from the middle tier. "There's simply no reason to keep going over it, since we lived it. That's the problem with mortals and their ulcers or even their stress levels going out the roof. They worry themselves silly over things that have already happened and can't be changed. That's why you're so good at your gift of healing by using your intuition." A long sigh escaped her. "How would you have helped the situation if a mortal had come into your shop and was blackmailing me?"

"Easy. Give them a forgetful potion," I said.

"Correct. But as you see, she's not alive."

I could see exactly where Eloise was going with this. "But the boyfriend is alive. All he knows is he was swarmed with insects."

She laughed. "Did you see how well the teens created the scene so we could escape? I should never have taken my cloak off."

"I need to go see him to give him a forgetful potion." I knew she was telling me I needed to do it without her actually saying it. "And I need to find where Roma stored all the information she'd been collecting."

"Yes." Eloise picked up the teapot again. "Tea?"

"Yes, please." I eased back in the chair with my hands on my stomach, calculating my next move before the Little One made an appearance in the world.

After I finished drinking my tea, we got up and decided to take a walk through her garden. Eloise gave me a basket so I could pluck whatever herbs I needed.

"You seem deep in thought." Eloise finally broke the silence.

"I've been reading Darla's journals from when she was pregnant with me."

I walked down each aisle, taking some rose petals, moonflower, mandrake root, seaweed, shrinking violet, dream dust, fairy dust, magic peanut, lucky clover, steal rose, and spooky shrooms, all of which I was low on in the storage room of the shop.

Eloise's garden was like a fairy tale. Every row was neatly planted. Each herb name was written on little wooden signs.

"Oh yes. I remember those nine months very well. The good and the bad." She looked over the singing petals. "I have to thin them out weekly, or they start to take over my thoughts."

They hummed as Eloise cut them and placed them in her basket, and I knew she'd take them to the various shops to distribute them.

In most cases, the owners would keep them in their shops because their harmony sounded like music playing over speakers, and their beauty was pleasing to the customers' eyes. Of course, the customers had no idea the beautiful harmony was coming from the flowers.

"I have been emotional lately and having nightmares. I don't think they are about what's happened with Roma, because the nightmares are about me holding a baby, and the baby needs food." I fiddled with the loose handle on the basket. "I wonder if, deep down, I'm questioning how I'm going to be a mom with parts of Darla and parts of this world. I know Darla did everything she could for me growing up, and she always taught me about death, but I want her here now more than ever."

A lump formed in my throat. Quickly, I tried to swallow it down before the tears started to tickle my sinuses and find their way up to my eyes.

"June," Eloise whispered my name and dropped the basket. "You know."

I nodded, not saying a word as the tears dripped down my cheeks. I knew and understood Darla's journal entry in which she'd written that she knew she wasn't going to see me grow into my greatness—into the spiritual life.

"Is that why she did everything she could to teach me about homeopathic cures? Did she do all the business stuff and learn all of it just because she knew she wasn't going to live long enough to show me when I needed it?" I questioned everything Darla had done for me. "Every dollar she made, she put into perfecting the lotions she had so it would be a good start for me."

Memories of my past flooded my mind. I recalled Darla sitting at the old kitchen table that we'd picked up from the side of the road in someone's garbage. Darla had used empty cardboard food boxes to fold up and place under the uneven table legs. But she sat there for hours upon hours, writing in that journal.

"Many times, I wanted to rip up the journal. Even burn it." My chest heaved with each deep breath I tried to take, but Little One was perfectly positioned under my ribs to make it hard for me to breathe. "Oscar and I tore up the house, looking for it, when she went to the flea market. We figured she kept it with her at all times."

"Aren't you glad she did?" Eloise knew how to turn it around in such a positive way.

"I am." I used the leaf of one of the drowsy daisies to wipe the tears off my face because it was Darla's favorite flower, and it felt like her hand on my cheek. "I'm so grateful to have it. But I hate that she knew she wasn't going to be here with me today." I looked at Eloise. "Why did you tell her about her fate?"

"Having a best friend who is a mortal is hard, June." She took another drowsy daisy and used it to wipe my other cheek. "You will find out, since Adeline is your best friend. They ask very deep questions when they get a feeling. More women than men. It's your duty to tell the truth in a loving manner. So when Darla had to know if you were going to be like her or us, I told her the answer she was seeking. But she didn't drop it from there."

"I don't know if I'm ready to hear this." I gulped. "There's too much going on, and I need to use what energy I have left to help Dr. Sebastian before Little One gets here."

A piece of Mr. Prince Charming's fur floated into the air. By the position of the sun, I knew it was time for me to go. I still needed to get him to Petunia to get checked out, and Oscar would be wondering exactly where I was, if Sonny hadn't already called him.

"You know I'm always here. I will tell you I did promise Darla that once you got to Whispering Falls, I'd always keep you close."

Eloise picked up the basket, and I picked up mine before I headed down the gravel sidewalk that led out of Eloise's garden.

CHAPTER SEVEN

I t was easy to lose track of time when using my spiritual gift and especially traveling between time with Eloise. I'd found that when either she or Aunt Helena did that with me in tow, time sped up, making it much later than I had anticipated.

Mr. Prince Charming led the way through the woods and around many of the treehouse rooms that belonged to Whispering Falls's only hotel, Full Moon Treesort. They were neat rooms that were built into the trees, making your stay in Whispering Falls a very different and magical getaway.

"You can feel the magic this afternoon," I told Mr. Prince Charming as he put us on the shortcut leading to the back of Glorybee Pet Store, owned by Petunia Shrubwood.

Glorybee happened to be the most popular shop in Whispering Falls. Who didn't love all the animals in there?

Customers and their animals were welcome. Everyone was welcome, even the critters Petunia could communicate with using her gift of being the local animal spiritualist. Every time I noticed her talking to an animal, I couldn't help but wonder who the animal was. When some people didn't cross over, they would take on the form of a certain animal and seek out Petunia to help them. Today, I wondered who the squirrel was because I could see Petunia up at the register with a squirrel on her shoulder as she talked to a bird that sat on top of the counter.

She had no problem with customers seeing her talking to the animals because they had no idea they were talking back to her. As I saw it, the customer figured she was just a woman passionate about her shop. And they would be right.

"Mr. Prince Charming." Petunia's words seemed to curl around him like a warm blanket. He had jumped onto her counter and dragged his tail under her nose. "I've been waiting for you."

Baby Orin bolted from clear across the store when he saw Mr. Prince Charming. I winced when I noticed he had a handful of hair from Mr. Prince Charming.

I wasn't sure why Petunia and Gerald, Petunia's husband, never corrected the toddler.

There was no doubt the entire village spoiled Baby Orin. He was the first baby in the village, and we all took our turns with him.

The village had gone years without a baby, and when Orin was born, we were beside ourselves. But now that he was walking, running, and saying a few words, he was a little on the rambunctious side and needing a little correcting. But I didn't dare say anything to Petunia.

After all, she was a dear, loving soul who cared for everyone and every creature.

"Orin, honey, be nice to the kitty. He's a good cat." Orin had grabbed a fistful of Mr. Prince Charming's hair before Petunia gently took his hand off of my fairy god cat. "It doesn't look like he's got too much more to lose."

She picked Orin up and propped him up on her hip. He turned on her and grabbed her long, messy updo, tugging on it, causing her head to tilt to the side as she talked to me.

"What on earth, June?" she questioned.

"That's why we are here." I wanted to tell her thanks to Orin, but instead, I smiled. "I've been finding large clumps of hair all over the cottage."

"Oh that." She waved it off. "He's going to be fine. It's all about Little One. He's worried Little One is going to be like Orin." She grimaced at the tot, who was going after a customer's dog.

She took off like a jet, and the squirrel scampered off and up the live tree planted in the far back corner of the shop. The bird disappeared into Petunia's messy updo, where I was pretty positive its nest was located, because several sticks protruded from the back along with the bird's tailfeather.

"You don't ever have to be worried about Little One." I picked up Mr. Prince Charming, nestling him against my chest and letting him nuzzle in my neck. "Oscar or I would never let anything hurt you. You forget," I whispered in his tiny cat ear, "I am half mortal, and I discipline."

Mr. Prince Charming purred happily until Orin was at my legs.

"Cat! Me want cat! Cat! Gimme! Gimme!" he screamed with his hands fisting and unfisting in the air toward Mr. Prince Charming.

"Orin," Petunia singsonged. "Look what Mommy has." She pulled a sucker out of her hair and held it out for him.

Quickly, he forgot about my cat and darted back to his mom.

"I'll never let him get ahold of you again." Once again, I made a promise to Mr. Prince Charming as I wondered exactly what Petunia was going to do with that boy of hers.

Petunia led Orin over to the tree and sat him up against the tree's trunk. I could have sworn I noticed the leaves shake and draw in away from the boy's reach. The animals scattered to the top branches. It was like no one was safe around him.

"Now, back to what I was wondering. Are you okay? You seem . . . a . . ." She waved her hands around me. "Ultraviolet."

I stood there as her eyes took in more of the aura my body was letting off.

"No surprise." I rolled my eyes. "Stress, nightmares—you name it, I've got it." I didn't go into it because Little One started to tumble around, letting me know it was time for supper. "But if you're sure Mr.

Prince Charming is okay, then I've got to run and check on Faith. She's been at the shop all day."

"He's fine." One of her brows rose. "But you are not."

"I'm good!" I waved bye to her and kept a close eye on Orin as Mr. Prince Charming and I headed out of the shop so I could get my fairy god cat away from harm if Orin did try to run after him.

Mr. Prince Charming bolted down the street, straight to A Charming Cure, with me following close behind. The day was slipping by so fast, and with so many things that'd happened, I was ready to get the shop ready for tomorrow and call it a day.

"Yoo-hoo! June!" Chandra Shango, owner of A Cleansing Spirit Spa, wiggled her fingers in the air. "How was your doctor's appointment?"

I wondered who had told her I had an appointment. It was always challenging to figure out how the gossip was spread throughout a spiritual community, with everyone having various gifts, and mind reading was one of those.

"It went well." I did love Chandra. She was always so perky and really did enjoy her job as a manicurist. "New turban?" I questioned the head covering I hadn't yet seen.

"This." She patted her thick fingers around it and raked the edges of her short raspberry hair peeking out from underneath of it. "It is adorable, don't you think?"

She moved her head from side to side so I could look at the light-blue turban with white clouds printed on the fabric.

"A spiritual traveling salesman came through while you were gone, and it was perfect for my summer sale display." She twisted her plump body to look at her own shop window, where she'd taken cotton material to make big fluffy clouds with a huge rainbow underneath. Each color of the rainbow had the name of one of the fingernail polishes she created in her shop. "Did you see my nails?"

She stuck her hand out, and I took a closer look at her painted nails. Each one looked exactly like her display.

"Tell me, do we know when Little One will make the special appearance?" She took my hands in hers in a loving fashion, but when she flipped them over to get a look at my palms, since she was a palm-reading spiritualist, I slowly withdrew them.

"We don't. But I think soon." I squeezed out a smile and didn't call her out on trying to read me, which was against the rules. "I've been gone all day, and I must go check on Faith."

"I can't wait for your shower," she called after me. "You're going to love it!"

If Oscar and I weren't careful and gave in to all the excitement swirling around about our baby, Little One was going to turn out just like Orin. And I didn't want that, I thought to myself when I made it up the steps and noticed the hole where the toddler had pulled the big chunk of hair from Mr. Prince Charming.

The shop had seen its last customer of the day, so when I entered, I flipped the sign over to Closed and walked back to talk to Faith. She and Mr. Prince Charming were having a moment, so I took my time walking through the shop to see exactly what the big sellers had been.

"Everything is out." Faith shrugged. "I even had to get some things from the back."

"The sale was good." I looked around and grinned. "This is great. I don't think I've seen a sale go this well in the last seven years."

"Seven years?" Faith's jaw dropped. "You've been here seven years?"

"It's hard to believe." I was pleased to see the men's items were low as well. I pointed at the display in disbelief.

"It was interesting with the customers' husbands today. Instead of sitting on the benches between the shops, they actually came in. I took the opportunity to really focus on them and get them interested in your line of the men's products." She walked over and stood in front of the display with me and rocked back on her heels.

"You did a fantastic job." I gave her a hug. "I can't thank you enough for watching the shop for me."

Little One kicked and kneaded my stomach when I came into contact with Faith. It made me pause.

"Faith," I said after she put her hand on my belly and Little One pushed a little hand out. It was so odd. I lifted my shirt over my belly. I could see all five fingers.

"Oh!" Faith gushed and put her hand on the baby's.

"I think Little One has just told me who our nanny needs to be." I looked up and started to cry.

"June, are you . . ." Faith raised her hand to her chest, and tears welled up in her eyes.

"I don't think I'm telling you. I know Little One is telling us." It seemed a little presumptuous on my part to assume Faith could do such a job along with her editor-in-chief job at the Whispering Falls Gazette and her part-time job at Wicked Good Bakery, where she helped her sister deliver the special orders. "Do you think this is something you'd be able to do?"

"Are you kidding me?" Her hands flew to her mouth. Her eyes looked down at my belly. "I've been having a strong feeling about it, but my ability to see into the future of an unborn spiritualist has proven to have its limits. I'd be delighted to!"

"It would be about four days a week. Oscar will have off a couple of days, and I'll take off a day a week, which would leave Little One coming to work with me one day." I wanted to make sure she knew exactly what I'd planned for my schedule so she could sit down and decide if she really wanted the job.

"Great!" She bounced on her toes with so much glee on her face. "When Little One is napping, I can get all the Whispering Falls Gazette finished, and since it's all in whispers, I can collect information throughout the day like I do now. As for the deliveries for Raven, those are already three days a week, so I can coordinate with the various shops we deliver to."

"I have a sneaking suspicion you already knew this was coming, even though you claim you haven't gotten a clear signal."

A sidelong glance from me was enough to crack her. "I might've put it in the breeze as a request." She giggled. "I've never had a request turned down, so I fully expected it."

"Then I'd better get going and get potions and cures made up to last for months, because I have a notion Little One wants to make an appearance sooner rather than later." I gave Faith a hug and sent her on her way.

Mr. Prince Charming curled up on the stool behind the counter while I walked into the storage room to retrieve a few of the items I was going to need so I could make up some very quick general homeopathic cures to restock the shelves so we'd be ready for tomorrow.

"We are going to have a busy day tomorrow." I talked to Little One as I picked out master root, Queen Elizabeth orris root, sweet grass braid, white sage flecks, pine resin, palo santo wood chips, and some myrrh resin. "These will do."

Most of the ingredients I'd picked were for general desires such as wealth, happiness, health, love, and healing.

It was much easier and quicker for me to have the base of the potions ready so I could easily add the exact ingredients they needed after I talked with the customers and got a good feel for my intuition about them.

"I bet you're exhausted." I ran my hand down Mr. Prince Charming's fur when I walked behind the stool. "I'm so sorry for the stress we've caused you about the baby."

The cauldron was still on when I went to put in the myrrh resin and wood chips. The mixture popped and cracked, sending up images of bees in the sparks. Immediately, I turned around and grabbed the apis bottle from the shelf and shook a couple of dashes of it into the pot.

"Apis." I was delighted when the images of the bees turned into buzzing, knowing the crushed bee was the perfect addition to the mix.

The bell over the door dinged.

"You forgot something?" I brushed my hands together and headed around the partition. "With all the excitement, you forgot to lock the door when you left."

I looked up and noticed it was Martha Perkins, the nurse from Dr. Sebastian's office.

"Martha." I wondered why she was here and how she'd found me. I put a smile on my face and reached into my bag to get my cell in case I needed to make an emergency call.

My bracelet warmed around my wrist. Mr. Prince Charming sat up.

"This town." Her mouth widened. She held a briefcase-looking bag at her side. "It's charming. I had no idea it was here, and the GPS…" She picked up one of the few bottles on the display counter closest to her. She slowly unscrewed the top and brought the lotion up to her nose. "Forget using GPS. It's like the town disappears once you get closer."

"I've always said the curvy roads from here to Locust Grove throw off all the satellites that work with GPS." I rubbed my charm bracelet to tap into my intuition. "We are closed but reopen in the morning."

I put my hands out, gesturing for her to go as I walked toward her to take her to the door. Mr. Prince Charming jumped off the stool and bolted in between me and Martha once we were close enough.

"Now that I'm here to let you know your test results, I might as well look around." She slid to the right, bypassing us and taking a cookie from the plate on the table next to the door.

"You didn't have to drive out all this way to tell me about results. You could've called." I opened the door of the shop so it was open for a quick getaway. "Why don't I bring you some samples to my next visit. You can see we sold out of a lot of items today. I'm trying to get some restocked, but I'm tired and hungry. Little One is definitely starting to wear me out."

She slowly turned to look at my belly.

I gulped.

"I love this one." She still had the bottle with the lemongrass lotion in her hand.

Immediately, I felt no intent to harm from her. My intuition chimed when she once again unscrewed the lid to take another smell.

She was there to seek some sort of answers and gather information. Her mind was full of puzzle pieces of information, though I was unable to tap into those.

"If you would like that, I'm more than happy to get you a brand-new one ready for you to take home tonight." With any luck, she'd agree, and I had a plan to put in place.

She hesitated.

"It'll only take a second, and while I do that, you can look around while you tell me the results." I had a feeling she was there about the murder, but she was not necessarily the murderer.

"That would be wonderful." She moved around the shop with a stern face, picking up various bottles while nibbling on her cookie.

Mr. Prince Charming darted under each table near Martha as though he were keeping a close eye on her.

The yellow bottle on the shelf glowed, letting me know Martha's favorite color was yellow, and the lemon scent she smelled was completely her doing. All the cures had no smell, but when found by the correct recipient, they took on the owner's favorite smells, sometimes even food.

"I love anything with lemons in it, but since I've been pregnant, I've been unable to eat anything sour." I shrugged and took the bottle from the shelf, keeping her in my peripheral vision as I walked around the counter to get the cure made for her and get out of her what she knew.

I slipped my bag off the back of the stool and took it with me and dug Madame Torres out.

Her face floated in the water. Her cheeks puffed out like she was about to throw up. Her pale face was sort of a green-and-gray-mixed color, and her eyeshadow had dulled.

"How dare you keep me in there all day?" she snarled. "You've given me seasickness and claustrophobia." She groaned, the color coming back to her face once I sat her next to the cauldron.

"I need a fast-acting truth serum." I didn't have time to look it up in Darla's journal, though I knew she had one in there that took a few hours to work.

Madame Torres disappeared, but words scrolled like the windows on a slot machine up her globe until they settled on the right concoction.

"Flax seed. Good one." I plucked the ingredient from the shelf, knowing it would help with mental powers and the protection of children. Martha was around a lot of children, and I wanted them protected. "Wood betony." I dragged my finger down the line, and the bottle of lousewort warmed to the touch, letting me know it was the wood betony with a different name, kind of like a generic form a mortal pharmacist would use to replace a brand-name drug if the insurance didn't approve it.

The two worlds were very similar yet different.

After a few dashes of each ingredient, I knew it was time for the main one.

"Yerba dock wormwood." The words left my mouth, giving me a little ease in my soul.

The cauldron contents rolled and rolled, mixing the ingredients and causing them to foam up right to the edge without spilling over. The air circulated above the mix, creating the smell of hundreds of lemon trees before the cauldron shut off.

"Here we go." I held the yellow bottle over the cauldron, and the mixture magically found its way into the glass. I used a simple cork top to plug the contents inside.

"I was saying your results were just fine. And I went in to bill your insurance." I'd come out just in time, because Martha was about to walk behind the counter.

Mr. Prince Charming was on his hind legs, meowing his little heart out.

"Your cat can do many tricks. You must tell me how you taught him. My cat just lies around, waiting for me to feed her. She's not very good at catching mice either." Her eyes settled on the bottle. "I can smell the lemon."

"It's the perfect combination for you." I uncorked the bottle and dabbed a little on her wrist for her to smell.

I watched as she lifted her wrist to her nose, and her facial expression brightened. A big smile curled along her lips.

"You know, I've suspected something fishy is going on at Dr. Sebastian's office between him and Roma. I think she was trying to do something underhanded at the office. But I'm not entirely sure what it was." She started to ramble as the truth serum began to kick in. "But today when you were scheduled to come to the office and were the only patient he saw, I knew something was funny. So I went to the office." She trembled. "I saw the sheriff's department tape, but I simply walked under it and couldn't help but notice Roma's car was still in the parking lot. I walked back under the tape and went straight over there. Did you know the car she's driving isn't her car but is in her lousy boyfriend's name? So the sheriff is looking for a car registered to Roma. They think the killer stole her car, when the car she's been driving was right under their noses."

Martha threw her head back and laughed. The potion was kicking into high gear, and she talked faster than ever. Her hands flew all over the place as she told her story animatedly. Mr. Prince Charming's head moved about as he tried to keep up with Martha's movements, but he finally gave up and moseyed back to the stool, as he recognized I was in no danger and had the situation under control.

That was until the Karima sisters hurried into A Charming Cure through the open door.

"June." Constance Karima's eyes narrowed, boring into Martha. "Is everything okay?"

"Yes. Okay?" Patience had changed the outfit on the bag of flour to a onesie with ducks on it.

"What is that?" Martha wiggled a finger at the sack of flour and slurred her words.

"I might've given her too much yerba dock wormwood." I shrugged.

"Yack dacka what?" Martha cackled and smacked the sack of flour, knocking it out of Patience's hands and causing it to bust.

Flour flew all over the place, and once the cloud settled, I could see the film it left over all of the bottles, the floor, and the display table.

Constance fanned her hand in front of her, letting out a series of coughs.

"Oopsie." Martha sounded like a baby who'd just gotten caught doing something wrong. "Why on earth would you be carrying a sack of flour around dressed like a baby?"

Patience leaned in, giving Martha a good long sniff.

"Death." Her one word was so powerful.

"Are you sick?" Constance asked Martha.

"No. Are you crazy?" Martha shot back.

"Are you sure you're not dying?" Constance asked again. "Know someone dying?" She reworded her question.

"You are lunatics, but I like it!" Martha tried to snap her fingers, but they just wouldn't connect. "There's something weird going on around here." She wobbled from side to side. Her eyelids appeared to get heavy. "I think you poisoned me, because I know you killed Roma."

Martha fell to the floor. The three of us stood over her.

"Meow." A faint call from Mr. Prince Charming made us all look over at him.

Constance let out a tee-hee. "Look. He's smiling."

"Smiling," Patience repeated.

Before Patience and Constance could enjoy any more of Martha's current state, a puff of smoke filled the shop.

Three pairs of boots dangled just below the fog.

"Welcome to A Charming Cure," I said to the Order of Elders before I even saw their faces.

"Oh dear, you've done it this time." Mary Lynn nervously stroked the fox stole around her shoulders. Her silver curls were tucked tight to her head. Her four-foot frame was dressed in the usual black suit, the one she always wore when she came calling.

She looked down at Martha, who was now snoring so loudly that Mr. Prince Charming had curled up into a ball and covered his ears with one of his front legs.

"Yes, you have." Mary Sue, the brashest of the elders, stood next to Mary Ellen, who was the youngest and hippest of the three Marys.

All three stood there, looking down.

"Maybe it's not as bad as it looks." Mary Ellen put her hands on her slim hips. Her long black hair was pulled back in a low ponytail, her slim figure sleek in her black one-piece bodysuit.

Mary Sue took the toe of her shoe and gave Martha a gentle nudge on the leg.

"Yucka ducka wormwood," Martha muttered. It was the name of the special truth serum I'd given her, though she didn't say it correctly, but it was enough for the Marys to understand. Then she started snoring even louder.

All three looked up at me. All six eyes waiting as if they wanted an explanation.

"June, you know better," Mary Lynn, the quietest and the shyest one, scolded me in her super-sweet voice, making me feel more ashamed than in trouble.

"You've done it now." Constance turned and marched out the door with Patience on her heels.

I curled my lips in and pinched them shut. It was better to just stay silent than to argue with the Marys. It was already bad enough they were here.

"Well, clean this place up." Mary Sue, who was the Mary who took charge, flipped both wrists, making brooms and all sorts of rags appear. "We can go talk. Our little visitor will be out for a while."

Mary Ellen picked up Martha's bag off the ground. There were some papers sticking out from the side pocket.

"I'm sure it's my ultrasound," I guessed since Martha was there to give me my results.

"Hmmm." Mary Ellen tapped her pointy-toed boot. "Dr. Sebastian. We still have to deal with him."

"Don't." I put my hands out. "I'm working on this. I've been doing this for seven year s," I said, reminding them how I'd been somehow picked as the Chosen One by the spiritual world. "I've already talked to him and Eloise. While Martha was midrant from the truth serum, she told me some valuable information about the victim's car, and when Eloise and I went to the victim's house, we couldn't find the documentation that Dr. Sebastian claimed Roma was blackmailing him with."

"Technically, truth serum is against the rules with mortals." Mary Lynn was telling me something I already knew, but she continued, telling me why. "You are only supposed to read them and make them potions to make their lives better. Not potions to gain something." She drew her gaze back to Martha, who was so asleep that she was now drooling. "Like you have done to her."

"But you see, I haven't gone against the rules. I used the truth serum to find out what she knew after she claimed something fishy was going on. I think Martha read something she found in Roma's boyfriend's car about the spirit world. And…" I knew I was about to throw them a big one. It was my only Hail Mary. "If I'm the Chosen One, then I have to know exactly what she knows so that I can keep our spiritual world together, away from the mortal world finding out."

"Marys." Mary Sue gestured for them to speak in private.

I gulped and watched as the three of them floated up into the air to the far corner of the shop and whispered amongst each other.

"What is going on here?" Isadora Solstice and Oscar came rushing into the shop with the Karima sisters behind them.

"Ma'am." Oscar bent down when he saw Martha on the floor and tried to wake her.

"No use in doing that," I mumbled, knowing he was going to be furious with me. "She's out. Yerba dock wormwood," I said, only to be met with gasps from him and Isadora.

"I told you she'd done it now." Constance was pleased with herself.

"Yep. Done it now." Patience wrung her hands.

"Not all is lost." Mary Ellen descended. She patted my belly.

"The Marys are here?" Oscar looked down at me with furrowed brows before he ran his hands through his hair. "What else did you do?"

"I sorta happened upon a murder, and Dr. Sebastian is a spiritualist. He's in trouble because I think he's at the top of Sonny Butcher's suspect list." Now I was starting to worry. Little One had stopped moving again.

Though Dr. Sebastian said everything was all right, I still worried.

"No wonder Sonny's been calling me all day. I've not had a chance to return his call." Oscar looked at the Marys. "Can I speak to you outside?" he asked them. "In private." He directed that toward me so I wouldn't follow.

Isadora and the Karima sisters stood over Martha like they'd never seen anyone snoring so much.

"She's spitting." Isadora was mesmerized by the drool.

"Mortals do that when they are sleeping really well." I made a simple comment, opening the door for Izzy, short for Isadora, to sweep across the room.

Her hazel eyes looked me over. She pushed her long blond hair away from her face before she took the red-and-white polka-dotted cloak from around her shoulders. She had on a black blouse with a black A-line skirt. The laced-up, pointy black shoes that most of us wore completed her usual look.

Once she reached me, she twirled around. She tossed the cloak into the air in front of her. It opened like a parachute and gently fell to the ground, covering Martha as if she were a corpse.

"Is she dead?" My jaw dropped.

"No, dear. Just going home, where she will wake up in the morning and not even know where yesterday went." Isadora drummed her fingers together as she counted. "One, two, three, mute you be."

The cloak snapped up into the air and found its way back around Izzy's shoulders, where it lay perfectly.

Martha was nowhere to be seen.

CHAPTER EIGHT

When I'd seen the Karima sisters rush out of A Charming Cure when Martha passed out and the Order of Elders showed up, I knew Oscar wasn't going to be happy with me.

I didn't need my intuition to tell me he was questioning why I'd not gone to him first thing after Roma was found dead. And when I finished telling him about Eloise's and my going to Roma's motel room, I thought he was going to lose his mind.

"You're pregnant." Though he didn't yell, the words did seethe out of his gritted teeth as he stomped back and forth in our family room. "Don't you know it's different now?"

I tucked one of the couch pillows under my arms and held it tight against Little One and me. If he was going to yell at me, I didn't want the baby to hear. Mr. Prince Charming already had a scowl on his face, just waiting to pounce on Oscar.

"I had Mr. Prince Charming with me," I repeated when there was a window of opportunity when Oscar had come up for air during his lecture.

"You have to think of others and not just yourself. That's my baby too." He jutted his pointer finger at me. "I don't care if you had a cat there. That's my kid."

"It's also mine, and do you honestly think I'd ever put us in danger?" I questioned him and held up my hand for him to hush while I said my piece. "Eloise was there. Your aunt, who is worlds smarter than we are when it comes to this world we are living in. Dr. Sebastian was there just in case something went wrong with the baby." I wagged a finger when he went to protest. "And Sonny was there. He would never let anything happen to me."

Oscar stared at me in silence. He bent down, curling his hands over his head, and brought his head between his knees.

He screamed in pain before he looked up at me with tears in his eyes.

"Don't you know how much I love you? This is our baby. Our love." He stood up, walked over to me, and bent down in front of me, taking the pillow away. He placed both of his hands on Little One. "Don't you know how much I have to keep you two safe? You're my world."

Gently, I took his head and held it against my stomach, trying hard to console him. His worry and hurt were like electricity in my veins. When he hurt, I could feel it to my core. It was a gift I'd always had with Oscar long before we were married.

"I'll be safe. But, Oscar…" I took my finger and put it under his chin to lift his head up to look at me. "You were warned before we got married that I was the Chosen One. We didn't really know what that was, but as the years have ticked by, it's become apparent that I'm to be involved with keeping our world a secret. As well as our home here in Whispering Falls. Whether I'm pregnant or not, that is my calling. We accepted that."

I forced him to remember all the ceremonies and the titles I'd held over the years and all the crimes I'd helped him solve.

"I just can't accept you doing that anymore." He stood up with a determined look on his face. "I came to an agreement with the elders, but I'm not going to let this happen. You are no longer allowed to be the Chosen One."

As much as I wanted to jump up, fist my hands, and throw a hissy fit, I knew Oscar was just speaking out of fear. His anxiety was coursing through him. His body was being fueled by it.

"What was your agreement?" I asked in a calming voice and pushed up off the couch.

"I told them I would call Sonny back and be put on the case to help him. At that point, I'd figure out all the mortal clues, while having you go into the spiritual part of it to figure out what Roma knew about us and whether it was any other spiritualist who killed her." He followed me into the kitchen, where I took a box of Ding Dongs out of the cabinet and took two out.

I handed him one and peeled the foil back. It was time to sink my teeth into my delicious stress relief and let my normal mind take over so I could come up with a plan to suit all parties, mainly Oscar.

"I think that sounds like a very reasonable plan. But to make it better, what if I come up with answers before the baby shower? That way…" I spoke louder so he wouldn't try to speak over me. "I can see what I can do before Little One gets here. Dr. Sebastian already told me the tests he had me do came out perfect, and the Little One is acting just like a spiritualist baby reacts at the end of the birth term."

Oscar's face shot up. His mouth formed into the biggest smile.

"Spiritualist? June, is Little One a spiritualist?" The excitement from hearing the wonderful news most definitely had overridden any doubt in his mind that I would ever put myself in harm's way.

"That's what the report said." I walked over to my bag, which was sitting on the counter, and took out all the papers I'd secretly swiped from Martha's bag before the Marys took it. I thumbed through them, only showing Oscar the printout from the machine with the images of a very healthy little spiritualist.

CHAPTER NINE

I f there was ever a better time to believe Little One was probably going to be a spiritualist, it was after I showed him the ultrasound and mentioned that Dr. Sebastian had commented on Little One's infrequent movement being, in fact, the same way spiritualist babies acted. Oscar looked as though he was pleased and really wanted the baby to be full spiritualist. I didn't tell him that we weren't certain, but it was enough for him to agree to my spending time helping out our world and clearing Dr. Sebastian's name as well as getting his insurance straight with the villages.

There was one person I knew who had contacts all over the various villages across the spiritual world that could get a bogus spiritual world insurance company up and running as quickly as a cloak could be tossed over her shoulders—Aunt Helena.

"Let's go." I hurried Mr. Prince Charming out the door before Oscar was out of the shower. If I was going to get back in time to open the shop, I had to get to Hidden Hall early.

It was so early that the moon was hanging in the dark sky, and the teens were still out, messing around—only a few, though. They teased Mr. Prince Charming along the way until he actually swatted one then trotted off with dignity.

"I told you guys to leave him alone," I said as I parted the wheat stalks in the field I had to walk deep into to find a wood post with multiple arms pointing in all directions to the various colleges at Hidden Hall.

Mr. Prince Charming darted ahead of me and waited patiently at the bottom of the sign.

"Eye of Newt Crystal Ball School, Tickle Palm School, Intuition School," I read carefully and slowly because some of the students at the university loved to be pranksters, and right before you touched the name you wanted to visit, they'd switch it on you so fast that you ended up going the wrong way. "Intuition School." I smacked it really quickly.

The wheat field opened to make a path that was perfectly manicured and led me straight to where I needed to go.

"Mewl, mewl." Mr. Prince Charming did a complete figure eight. He did that when he wanted me to slow down, and he was right. Little One had been very active that morning and was probably a little hungry.

I reached down into my bag and pulled out a Ding Dong, the exact thing Little One and I needed. Well. . .it made me feel better to think the Little One needed it.

"There. Ready?" I looked at Mr. Prince Charming, who delightedly darted down as the path gained momentum clearing in front of us.

We came to a small yellow cottage that had window boxes under each window that overflowed with geraniums, morning glories, petunias, moon flowers, and trailing ivy that left an explosion of colorful rainbows that left me speechless every time I saw it.

It was the classroom where I'd learned to hone my spiritual gift a few months after I'd moved to Whispering Falls. It was also where I had become friends with Raven and Faith Mortimer.

The real thing that touched my heart for the classroom was when they'd asked me to teach a year ago. I had no idea how fulfilling it was to pass on my skills to eager young intuition spiritualists. Honestly, I'd thought a lot about how my child would benefit and have an amazing jump in the spiritual world by being born of the world. Then I got pregnant. Though I'd never told Oscar, I was very excited to teach Little One as well as learn how to be an amazing mom.

I passed by the window of the classroom quickly so I wouldn't be seen. Most students and faculty knew me and my aunt Helena, who was the dean.

Mr. Prince Charming knew his way around here, like he did everywhere he went.

"We've been waiting to see you. And I mean see," I told the apparition walking next to Mr. Prince Charming.

"Dang, I thought I could get to Helena before you." Gus Chatham, Aunt Helena's assistant, loved to use his teleporting gift to mess with us every time we came to Hidden Hall. "Can I interest you in a cocktail at Black Magic Café?"

"Cocktail? You mean some sort of crazy drink that would take my saliva and tell you so you can tell Aunt Helena what sex the baby is?" I tapped my temple. "Gotta be smarter than the Chosen One." I winked, teasing Gus.

It had been our thing since I met him seven year s ago. He loved trying to throw curve balls to create a little fun, but he was always there when we needed him.

"Where is she?" I asked as I passed Once Upon a Spell Library on the left and the girls' dorms on the right. Straight ahead was the building with all the teachers' offices, including Aunt Helena's.

"She's in the childcare center." Gus finally appeared. His shaggy ash-blond hair was tamer than usual, but his lanky six-foot body was still dressed like a surfer guy. He shuddered. "There's a lot of really talented kids out there now. You thought I was a good clairvoyant medium—wait until you see the next generation."

"Gus." I stopped him. "You don't have to tell me that she's in there checking out our future leaders when I know she and Oscar have concocted a plan for Little One to come here. I have some news about that." I knew it was going to be a blow to everyone there who was anticipating my bringing the baby there. "I've got an in-home sitter."

"I will not be around when you tell her that. Do you understand what I'm saying?" he questioned with a frightened look on his face.

"I know Aunt Helena can be a bit much, but she'll be fine. Besides, she's always said that having the baby at home was best, but we all know I can't work from home."

Though I had thought about turning the storage room in the back of A Charming Cure into a makeshift nursery. The idea went out the door after I was swamped one day and never even checked on Mr. Prince Charming. That was when I knew I had to get childcare.

"Fine." Gus wiggled his finger in front of him. "You can follow Mr. Prince Charming. He knows the way."

"Wow." I laughed. "You really don't want to be near us when I tell her."

"Nope." He swung his hands in front of himself like an umpire calling a baseball player who'd slid to home base safe. "No way. I've been around here, and I know what she's been up to."

"What if I meet you at Potions, Wands, and Beyond afterward? We can look at all the baby stuff," I suggested.

"Oh yes! Now you've made my day," he gushed before his figure pixelated and dissolved, leaving me to my own devices to face Aunt Helena.

The childcare center was located in a building shaped like a shoe, like in the fairy tale. It was a five-story shoe with a different age group on each level. Once the child reached five years old, they were eligible to attend their village's regular school while their parents came to work.

It was no different from mortal school and parents who worked at a university or in regular jobs. The only differences were classes. Mortal kindergarten children learned their ABCs, while spiritualist children were taught the potion table of ingredients.

Mr. Prince Charming and I walked up the steps to the first set of shoelaces and opened the door, which was the bottom part of the tongue of the shoe. It was all very strange. When you opened the door, it was like any other preschool. The office was in the open area, where the director of the childcare acted like a guard.

"May I help you?" she asked, standing up. The woman had black hair pulled up into a tight bun on the top of her head and wore a pair of black-rimmed glasses, a blue-and-white-striped dress that went down to her ankles, and a pair of tennis shoes—no doubt the perfect outfit to be running after children all day.

"Hi, I was wondering if Helena Heal is here."

The woman's eyes popped wide open. She knew exactly who I was.

"Yes. I'm June, her niece." I patted my belly.

"Yes. Of course you are. We are so excited to welcome your Little One here." She grabbed a file from her desk and opened it. "Have you seen Dr. Sebastian lately?" she asked with her pen in her hand, ready to write my response.

Have I?

Instead of answering her question so she could document my answer, I gave her an answer that practically sent her to her knees.

"I'm here to let you know Little One won't be coming to childcare here. We have hired an in-home sitter." My words literally made her legs buckle. She dropped the file when she went to grab the edge of the desk to steady herself.

"Are you okay?" I asked.

"I-I'm. . ." she stammered and looked at me with fear in her eyes. "You can find your aunt right over there."

I followed her nervous gaze to an office with a huge window that looked out into the open area.

"Thanks," I said in a cheerful manner. I tapped on the window when I saw Aunt Helena hovering over a baby crib. I couldn't stop smiling when I saw her pointy red-toed boots.

She smiled widely and waved me in as she descended down. Her red hair was gorgeous and ran down her back. Her emerald eyes matched her cloak of choice today.

"What a joy." She threw her hands together. Her long fingernails clicked. She swept across the room. "I'm so glad you are here. Though I heard the Order of Elders came for a little visit."

"That's why I'm here. I wanted to run by all the clues to see if you had any insight so I can get this thing wrapped up before the baby shower." I looked around the room. "New room? I smell the paint."

"The only baby going in here is this one." She put her hand on my stomach then suddenly jerked up to look at me. She gasped. "No. This will not do. The baby will come here for me to look after."

"I guess you know?" I looked between her and my belly.

"And Faith Mortimer? She's a baby herself," Aunt Helena cried. Thunder clapped outside of the building. The windows shook. Her anger would be felt all over Hidden Hall, and I'd be the bad guy.

She bent down and started talking all sorts of gibberish to my stomach. Little One rolled and moved—before hitting my bladder a few times.

"No. No. No." Aunt Helena stomped over to the crib. "This is your crib. You will come here and do as we say!"

"Aunt Helena!" I hollered. She and the baby both seemed to be having some sort of fit. "I don't know what is going on, but I will not tolerate you telling my baby what is what. That's for me and Oscar to decide."

"And that is Darla coming out in you!" She pointed her long finger at me. "I warned Otto of this when he married the mortal."

I gulped. My eyes lowered. I knew there'd been tension between Darla and Aunt Helena, but I never questioned it. Darla had alluded to it in the journal, but it wasn't something I wanted to bring up, especially since Aunt Helena was my only living relative. But now with my bringing the baby into the world, I desperately wanted Darla here.

Instead of standing there any longer, I turned on the balls of my feet and walked out of the room. I found the director of childcare huddled in the corner of her office with her knees up to her chest.

"We will not be bringing our child here." I picked the file up off the floor and ripped it in half then left it on the desk.

The sunny day had suddenly turned dark and gray. The thunder and lightning had definitely been brought on by Aunt Helena's anger. I was angry too.

"This is our baby." I stalked down the street with the rain pouring down on Mr. Prince Charming and me. "I will not let anyone, not even a spiritualist, tell me what to do. Even a head one." My hands were fisted.

Suddenly, an umbrella popped over our heads, dangling, with no visible person holding it.

"Thank you, Gus." I could feel him there. "I guess you've figured out the talk didn't go so well."

"I really shouldn't say a word." Every once in a while, the rain would shift with the wind, and an outline of his body could be seen.

"You don't have to. But I won't have her talk about my mother this way." It was rare that I called Darla my mother, since she only wanted to be called Darla, but she was my mom, and I needed her more than ever.

"You know, your mother stood up to her, too, and I'm sure that's what's made her so angry." Gus had never mentioned anything about Darla to me over the past seven years.

"You knew Darla?" I asked.

"Knew her? Dude, I had to tele back and forth between here and Eloise's just to see what they were up to. You know your aunt and Eloise…"

"Yeah, I already know they didn't get along." It was becoming very clear that this whole spiritualist life was starting to collide with my mortal values, leaving me a little unsettled.

Had I made the wrong decision to raise Little One as a spiritualist when I wasn't raised as one? I clearly didn't follow the rules or even know the rules, for that matter.

"There's just so many things we need to teach your baby at a young age that Helena is worried if she's not here to watch the progress, the baby will be confused when school starts. Sort of behind all the others. And there's never been a Heal that wasn't a leader." He tried to make a good case for Aunt Helena, but I also had a good case.

"I want my child to have a normal life." When I said the words, I knew it sounded ridiculous and mortal. "You know what I mean. I want Little One to have experiences like ballet or football, baby dolls or basketballs. Not just eye of newt and springler frog legs or potions and wands. A full life."

"Let me give you one bit of advice to chew on before you go." We stopped at the edge of the wheat field. The path back to Whispering Falls opened up before us. "You need to talk to Petunia. She's from a long line of spiritualists, and she's had a baby."

"A terror of a toddler." I hated to say it, but Orin was turning out to be hell on two feet.

"Regardless, there are things we must teach children born of two spiritual parents, or the baby will never make it in our world and might become one of *them*." Gus appeared. His eyes were dark with knowing.

"You mean a bad dark sider?" I'd only been around one really bad spiritualist, and I sure didn't want Little One to turn out like him.

"It's like when a mortal goes to what they call the wrong crowd." He gave me a sidelong glance. "Helena is worried you won't be aware of all the things the baby needs to learn. Those things are taught in the infancy stage. Not when they grow up to be a teen. Evil can creep into a baby's soul before the baby even knows what it is. You don't look like that's on your mind."

He stood over me with the umbrella, which I really appreciated, but I was already drenched.

"I've got an issue that I needed Aunt Helena's help with, and that's why I came here." I bit the inside of my lip and tried to come up with how I was going to get someone to create a fake insurance company so that when Martha or the police or the sheriff tried to look into Roma's claim when they figured it out—and I was sure they'd figure it out—someone from our world would be able to intercept those calls.

"What on earth is more important than the well-being of Little One?" Gus asked.

"Nothing, but since Little One isn't here, I have a lot of things to do, and solving a crime that would take down our world is one of them." It was more important than ever to get this fake insurance set up.

"What are you talking about?" he asked.

"These." I took the papers out of my bag and flipped through them as he continued to hold the umbrella up over us.

"Insurance the doctors fill out."

"How did you know?" I questioned.

"Umm… I'm the dean's assistant. Duh." He really sounded like his surfer-dude look. "They teach doctors that see mortal patients how to fake bills for spiritualist services. . ." His mouth opened then shut then opened again. "Are you telling me Dr. Sebastian didn't bill the insurance?" Gus's brow rose.

"Yeah, and the receptionist, the murdered one, Roma, well, her job is to file the insurance and take the co-pay. Apparently, after a spiritualist came in and she went to file the insurance, it came back that there was no such insurance company." As I talked, I could see the light bulb come on in his head as he put two and two together. "She went back through all the files and pulled them. Calculating over millions of dollars' worth of services."

"Oh no." Gus shook his head. "This is bad, June."

"It's more than bad. Roma was blackmailing Dr. Sebastian over it." I didn't have to finish my sentence.

"If the sheriff puts it together, Dr. Sebastian looks like the killer." Gus pulled his lips together as if he were thinking.

"Eloise and I went to her motel, where she lives with her boyfriend, and couldn't find any such evidence, so we believe it's in the car she was driving." I waved my hands so he didn't put too much emphasis on it. "I'm going to see the car today."

It was just one more thing on my to-do list.

"What I need from Aunt Helena is for her to create a bogus number with a spiritualist that will answer any claims if the police do find out about Roma looking into the cases and try to do a check on all of Dr. Sebastian's insurance filings." I moved my hand in the air like I could do air magic, which I wished I could do. "And I need her to wave her cloak magic over whatever paperwork there is to put that number on all of those claims."

"Can you give me an hour and let me see what I can do?" he asked.

I nodded with so much gratitude. "Yes."

"This is not anything to do with Little One. It has everything to do with us." He gestured between the wheat field and the university. "This could destroy us."

Gus disappeared.

I stood at the top of the path. My hair was matted to my face from the pouring rain. I was soaked to the bone, and I shivered, but my intuition told me my shaking wasn't from being cold.

CHAPTER TEN

The sun was bright over Whispering Falls. I didn't even dare look back at Hidden Hall once I got to the end of the path. Mr. Prince Charming darted ahead to do whatever it was he was going to do the rest of the day.

Before I could go to work, I knew I needed to change my clothes and dry my hair, thanks to Aunt Helena's tantrum.

Gus had given me a lot to think about, and from what I could feel, I needed to talk to Oscar about it. He and I had both agreed we'd raise the baby ourselves with our morals and not just the spiritual world's. It hadn't been easy for us to transition to who we really were, but we'd learned, and we were still learning how to maneuver our way around. We were fine. We'd never let anything happen to the baby.

Sonny Butcher's sheriff's car was parked in front of my cottage, and I found him and Oscar sitting at the table.

"June, what on earth?" Oscar jumped up. "Was it raining?" he asked and gave me a look of "Oh no" when he remembered he couldn't say anything about our life in front of Sonny.

"I went to see Aunt Helena at the childcare center. It was water day, and it got all over me when things didn't go so well." I grinned. "Hi, Sonny. You know kids and water. They can't stand to see an adult dry."

"I don't know kids, but I'll take your word for it." He shook his head. "How are you feeling?"

"I'm all fine. Thank you for letting Dr. Sebastian do the test on me, which confirmed we are good." I patted my belly. "I'm assuming you're here to ask for Oscar's help?"

"You've always had such a good insight." He nodded. "But he's not budging on this one."

"Why?" I turned my head to look at Oscar, flinging water.

"It's just too close to the baby's due date, and. . . Colton is out today, and I don't have the heart to call him in."

"You have others you can have work for you, and we need the extra money." It was my way of saying we needed to get this case wrapped up before the baby shower, and we'd agreed. What on earth had caused his change of heart?

"I know, but the more I thought about it while you were sleeping, the more I want to be closer to home."

"You've made him a softy," Sonny teased.

"Can I talk to you?" I asked Oscar and walked to the bathroom, where I had to get ready. I shut the door once he was in. "What happened? We agreed. What is going on around here? Dr. Sebastian is a spiritualist doctor, there's a murder, Orin is wild, Aunt Helena has lost her mind." I threw my hands up in the air. "I should've known things would start going south after they've been so good."

"June." Oscar took my hands. "I don't want anything to happen to either of us. What if I get killed trying to find a killer? If you weren't pregnant, maybe I'd put my life on the line. But we've got it good here. It's easy. A simple life we can enjoy with our family. Something neither of us had."

He made a good point.

"We won't have this spiritual freedom if I don't help solve the murder, and I need you in there to help me." I could feel the tension crawling across my forehead. "The baby is literally sucking the energy out of me, and we need to be a team."

Oscar let out a few long sighs as he appeared to be contemplating what I was saying, and he knew I was right as much as I knew it, but I could see his side as well.

"Get in there and work really hard to see what they know. I can use what little magic I have in me to sort out the findings so we can wrap this up by tomorrow night." I didn't have to plead anymore.

His eyes softened. He gave a slight smile and a few simple nods.

"I love you." He ran his hand down my face before he left the bathroom.

While the two of them celebrated Oscar agreeing to work a few extra days in Locust Grove with more coffee, I took a much-needed shower, a hot one at that. The chill had gone deep to my bones, and the water soothed the baby.

"Mewl, mewl." Mr. Prince Charming batted at the shower curtain. It was his way of telling me to get out.

I turned the water off and opened the curtain to grab my towel. With the towel wrapped around me, I slightly opened the door to hear what Sonny was saying about the case.

"We are looking at three people who had motive to kill her. She lives in a motel with her boyfriend, who is a huge activist. They travel from town to town to help spread whatever cause he wants to work with. She usually gets jobs in doctor's offices because she's got a two-year degree in business administration." Sonny was talking about Roma. "We have sent out some background checks on her and her boyfriend, but those won't be back for a few days."

"A few days?" I questioned and looked at Mr. Prince Charming. "We don't have a few days."

Mr. Prince Charming and I both eased back to the door to listen some more.

"We did pull up a police report where the night-shift manager at the motel had called the police about a domestic violence case against the boyfriend. Since it was Locust Grove Police, I have a call in to them to check in on that."

"You think it was a domestic-abuse murder?" Oscar asked.

"I think it's possible. Like I said, when we get the background check back, we'll be able to see if there is a pattern." There was a bit of frustration in Sonny's voice. "The problem is they've moved around so much in the last four years, it's hard to get the various reports tracked down."

That was where Oscar would be very handy. He'd be able to go to the Locust Grove Police Department and wave his wand around, which would turn up all the reports needed.

Too bad he just couldn't do it right there out of thin air—or anyone else I knew. So the boyfriend would definitely go on my list to see. I also had the papers I'd taken from Martha's bag.

Speaking of Martha, I wondered how she felt today and if she did remember anything.

"What about the scene of the crime?" Oscar asked.

"We got the dumpster moved to evidence overnight, and we took the tape down this morning so the doctor's office could reopen. After work, the nurse and doctor will be in to give full statements. I'll be asking them about any relationships they had with her. If she was happy. Those types of questions, because when we brought the boyfriend in, he said Roma and Martha didn't get along. When I asked Martha about their relationship at the scene before I talked to the boyfriend, she said Roma was wonderful and they had no problem." Sonny didn't sound as though he was convinced.

If that was the case, did Roma tell Martha about what she'd been finding out about the insurance, and that was why Martha knew about it? Did Martha know about the paper trail Roma had collected?

"We still haven't located her car. We'd like to find that. The boyfriend isn't cooperating on that end, which makes it very suspicious."

"What would you like me to do first?" I knew Oscar was ready for the task.

"I'd like you to go see the boyfriend and find out what all he's about. His relationship with her, whether or not he abused her. The things you get out of people. For some reason, people love to open up to you, and I'd like to get this case solved fast." I heard the chair legs scoot against the floor followed by footsteps. "Here's the address."

There were a few mumbled words between them that I couldn't make out before I heard Oscar tell Sonny he'd see him later.

I hurried across the hall to get dressed.

"I'm guessing I don't have to tell you what we talked about." Oscar let me know he knew I was eavesdropping. "I've made you a coffee and left you a Ding Dong."

"Thank you." I tugged a short-sleeved maternity tee over my head and slipped on a pair of jean leggings along with a pair of tennis shoes. I'd noticed my feet were starting to swell a little, and with my standing all day at the shop and needing to go to Locust Grove that afternoon to snoop, I'd figured I might as well be comfortable.

"Love you!" I hollered to let him know it was all good when he was walking out.

"I'll call you later." He shut the door.

"We've got work to do." I wiggled my brows at Mr. Prince Charming and headed down the hall to grab my coffee and Ding Dong.

First, I took Madame Torres out of my bag and tapped on her. "It's almost eight o'clock. You'd better be up," I said to her when her globe still had a moon floating in the water. "We've got work to do. Real detective work this time."

"Well, well, well." She appeared with a sarcastic look on her face. Her bright-red lips said, "I'm guessing you're needing my help since your aunt Helena went off the rails this morning." Madame Torres brought her fingernails up to her face and looked them over. "It's all the talk among the balls."

"I guess I'm needing your help because you are my crystal ball and I could find you a nice home as a paperweight." It was a threat, and she knew it was one I pulled when she had her sassy pants on.

Crystal balls only were visible to whom they were supposed to service. She could see me, and I could see her. No one else could see her, and if they did, they'd think she was a snow globe or a fancy colored ball.

"I'd like to see you try to give me away." She glared at me.

"Really?" I snapped back. "Try me!" I was in no mood for any sort of snarking familiars. "I'm going to have this baby soon. And I'm in no mental shape to take any lip from you. So get me the information on where Roma's car is located. I need to let Oscar know so it'll buy me time to get to the boyfriend's car."

I picked her up and threw her into my bag then put the strap over my shoulder so I could get down the hill to open up the store.

Of course, my actions were met with some mumbles and grumbles from Madame Torres since I did toss the bag into the passenger seat of the old El Camino since I would take it to Locust Grove that afternoon.

It was getting harder to walk down the hill, so driving was much easier. Instead of taking up a parking space in front of any of the shops, I parked in the parking lot next to Glorybee, where the Full Moon Treesort guests parked their cars, and walked across the street to A Charming Cure.

It was already shaping up to be a gorgeous day, and it looked as if we were already full of tourists. There were lines formed in front of many of the shops already. My heart sank when I didn't see anyone in line at A Charming Cure.

The purple-and-white wisteria vine was nice and perky, very pleasing to the eye. Then I noticed the shades of the display window were open.

I trotted up the steps and into the shop, where Faith Mortimer was working with a customer.

She and I waved, and I made my way back to the counter, wondering why she was here.

"June," she called in her sweet voice. "I heard that you've had a rough morning, and I finished all my deliveries for Wicked Good, so I thought I'd come and help out today and tomorrow."

"Faith, you are a good friend." Relief settled over me. She'd heard through the breeze everything that'd taken place that morning, and she knew how important it was for me to get to Locust Grove.

"I am warning you to be careful. The breeze only gave bits of information about the murder, and I can't help but worry about Little One and the impending arrival." A look of concern crossed her face. "And

Helena came to visit me. Boy, is she mad. I forgot what a hard teacher she was." Faith trembled. "Scary."

"Don't you worry about her," I assured her. "You will be Little One's nanny. I can promise you that." I hugged her. "But if I'm going to get a jump on this case, I'd better get going."

My bag glowed.

"I need to grab something in the back." I scampered to the back room and took Madame Torres out. "I hope you've got something."

She showed me a map and a bullseye on Nashville, Tennessee.

"That's where her car is located. The boyfriend doesn't want to tell them about his car because they stole it from a Nashville resident. The car is still parked behind the doctor's office. I suggest you check the trunk for the paperwork you need."

"Thank you." I kissed the ball.

"Gross. Yuck. Stop!" she yelled. "Don't get your slobber all over me!"

"See? Was it so hard to do me a favor?" I asked and stuck her back into the bag, escaping out the back door of the shop.

The street was buzzing with tourists, and it was so nice to see. As spiritualists, we had a hard time connecting to the warmer seasons when our real wheelhouse was the fall. The village council had been working really hard on making Whispering Falls a place tourists would visit all year round.

On my way past Glorybee Pet Shop, I noticed Mr. Prince Charming had taken the long way around to meet me at the green machine. Through the window, I could see Petunia chasing Orin around. He had a stick in his hand, no doubt from Petunia's hair, and was chasing after one of the hedgehogs that lived at the pet shop.

Petunia's forehead was deeply creased, and there was a fake smile on her face that told me she was trying to keep it together. It made me wonder if having Faith babysit Little One was a wise decision. I certainly didn't want the baby to turn out to be rambunctious and destructive.

Petunia caught my eye, and her shoulders drooped. She lifted her hands in the air and shrugged. Even though it was against the bylaws to read another spiritualist, you didn't need a good intuition to see Petunia was about at her wit's end.

I gave a slight wave so she wouldn't think I'd noticed the difficulty Orin seemed to be giving her and headed to the parking lot, where Mr. Prince Charming had already taken his spot on the dashboard.

My first stop would be the doctor's office, which had not yet opened. It was a good time to drive around back and look for the car Madame Torres had showed me in the crystal ball. The other papers had to be in there. The papers Martha had dropped were only the insurance claims to the fake account. Which reminded me that'd I'd not heard from Gus, which made me believe he couldn't talk to Aunt Helena.

Not that she wouldn't help, but she was too upset with me to be doing anything. At least, I hoped that was why he wasn't there.

"Are you ready?" I looked at Mr. Prince Charming, and I could have sworn he nodded.

CHAPTER ELEVEN

I t took very little time for me to get to the other side of Locust Grove because I knew the shortcuts through town.

"Good old Madame Torres," I whispered when I saw the exact car she'd shown me to be the boyfriend's car. "It's time to call Oscar."

I pulled my bag across the seat and took out the cell phone, then I hit Oscar's contact number, sending me straight to him.

"Are you okay?" was the very first thing he'd say to me since I'd been pregnant.

"I'm fine. Stop worrying about me," I said with a smile, thankful to have such a loving husband when Roma didn't even have that in a boyfriend. "I've got some news from Madame Torres."

"What's that?" he asked.

"She said Roma's car that the police are looking for is in Nashville." I wanted some time to break into the boyfriend's car. If they figured out from the boyfriend that she'd used his car and they got here right now, our world would be done.

"Did she give an address?" he asked. I kept my eye on the car and noticed a faint apparition.

"Gus," I whispered.

"Huh?" Oscar must've heard me.

"Nothing. I'm listening." I grinned when Gus appeared and waved a stack of papers in the air.

"I've yet to get into the computer system, since I just got here and have been saying hello to the others. Send me the address," he suggested. "Well, it's not going to help, because she sold the car, and they stole another one that's located behind the doctor's office."

"Here." Gus appeared in the passenger seat with the papers. "Car owner's information is in the glove box."

"What?" Oscar questioned.

"Yep. You'll be able to bring the boyfriend in on theft charges. All the information of the real owner is in the glove box," I repeated what Gus had told me so that they could get the boyfriend in and get rid of any notion of grabbing Dr. Sebastian, giving me some free time to get the insurance in place.

I told Oscar the make and model of the car before I hung up and drove around to the front of the doctor's office so the police wouldn't see me when they got there.

"She was definitely on the right path." Gus handed me a few of the papers with Roma's handwriting on them.

"She even had village names." Shock and awe came over me when I noticed she'd written down a lot of the western villages and some I'd traveled to. "She even marked dates of birth."

"That's not all. She also went as far as going back into Dr. Sebastian's travel log showing he didn't deliver babies for the spiritualists that came to see him. Nor did any follow-up. So when she did the research on the patients at the nearest hospitals to their village, there was no record of birth. Plus no midwife had any of the names." Gus's eyes darkened. "She talked to a lot of people, and. . ."

"So when I have Little One, who is going to help me deliver?" I knew it wasn't the right time to ask that, but I had to know if Dr. Sebastian didn't do it, then who did.

"The right spiritualist will be sent to you at the moment." He didn't make me feel better, just more anxious.

"What do you suggest we do about this?" I asked him.

"I suggest you go to the doctor's office and tell Dr. Sebastian what you found out. See if he can go through the files to correct any current patients while I get these back to Helena. She has no idea I took on this task."

Gus was really sticking his neck out for me and our world. Even though he should be working with Aunt Helena, he was doing a good thing, and I was sure she'd approve.

"Thank you, Gus." I put my hand out and placed it on his arm. "You're saving our world."

"I'm hoping Helena will get these insurance agents in place and a phone number put on the documents."

That was everything I wanted. I held my crossed fingers in the air.

"Do you think she'll do it?" he asked me with some worry on his face.

"If she knows our world is in danger." I nodded.

Just then, the sheriff's deputy drove past us and turned to go around the building.

"Showtime." Gus smiled, and it reached his eyes. "Now is the time to get in there with these while they take the boyfriend into custody. I made copies of the papers for you. I sent the originals to the dean's office."

"Let's hope they nab the boyfriend. He might know what's going on, and hopefully Oscar can be the one to question him, so we don't have to worry that the real sheriff will find out."

I knew it had to be hard on Oscar. He'd always taken pride in upholding the mortal law and spiritual law with morals and dignity. This was a clash between his two worlds, and that explained his hesitation to take the assignment when Sonny came to him. Now that we had a baby to think of, I had a feeling this was going to be Oscar's last case with mortal crimes here in Locust Grove.

Gus did his famous trick of disappearing without so much as an *adios*, leaving me to formulate the plan all alone.

"Fine." I shoved the papers into the bag and threw my cell phone in. "It's time to go tell Dr. Sebastian."

Mr. Prince Charming didn't bother lifting his head. He just gave me a few blinks and yawned before he went back to curling up and sleeping. It made me feel better. If he had gone in with me, I'd be on high alert that I was in danger.

There were a few pregnant patients in the waiting room, and when I saw Sylvia in there, my heart sank. I headed to the sliding receptionist window and ran a finger along the appointment book since no one was sitting at Roma's desk. My name magically appeared as an appointment for that exact time.

"Hi, Sylvia," I eased down into the seat next to her. "June Heal," I said to jog her memory.

"Yes. How is everything since, what, two or so days ago?" Her brows furrowed, and by her tone, I knew she thought something was wrong with the baby.

"It's all good. I'm here to talk to the doctor about insurance, of all things." I rolled my eyes.

"That's a pain." She laughed. She was dressed in a nice suit and carried a satchel. "You have no idea how much insurance is involved in IVF."

"Are you here for it?" I asked and almost suggested she come see me at A Charming Cure so I could get some intuitional reading on her and possibly help her out, if nothing other than a stress relief cream to help put her at ease. I'd seen so many of my customers who worried and worried about getting pregnant, but once they didn't focus as much on it, they ended up getting pregnant.

"Sylvia." Martha opened the door. She appeared well rested, which made me think she didn't have any sort of memory of what had happened last night. "Dr. Sebastian is ready to talk to you."

Mr. Prince Charming appeared at my feet and reached up with his paw to bat my bracelet.

"I guess I'll see you again." She stood up. "I didn't see your cat before."

I eyeballed Martha. When she opened the door was when Mr. Prince Charming showed up. I gulped and watched as Martha glanced at me and my fairy god cat before she looked down at the file in her hand.

"I rarely see the same patient twice in here since my schedule is so crazy. Good luck." Sylvia winked and smiled.

"Yeah. You too." I sighed and got lost in deep thought about how she must really feel seeing all of these women in the waiting room that were pregnant. It would be so hard, and I was really grateful to be blessed with Little One. "I guess you wanted to be in here."

Mr. Prince Charming was curled up at my feet. A few of the other patients noticed him and gave me a sweet smile. It opened up a conservation between all of us about how we all had different pets to introduce the babies to. A lot of the first-time moms gave advice on how to introduce the baby to the fur baby.

"June." Martha said my name like she had a sour lemon in her mouth. "Dr. Sebastian will see you in room four."

Oh, I knew room four.

"How are you today, Martha?" I asked as she took my blood pressure once she got me up on the table.

"I'm fine. The baby looked good in your test yesterday. Did Dr. Sebastian go over the results with you?" She looked in my file.

Her question was great. She had no memory of going into my file to find my address and showing up at the shop, where she claimed to want to deliver the test news in person, though we all knew better.

"He did. I'm so glad everything is all good with the baby." It was a huge relief, even though the test was bogus.

"What brings you in today?" She asked a very good question.

"I had some questions about the delivery." I shrugged and swung my legs.

She moved out of the way of my limbs and looked down. She grabbed one of my legs and took a look at it.

"Can you slip off your shoes?" She had a look of concern that worried me.

I did what she asked, and she began poking around my ankles.

"How long have you had this swelling?" she asked with even more concern in her eyes.

"I just now noticed it since you pointed it out." *Oh gosh. Now what?*

Mr. Prince Charming sat in the chair like a human. He kept his eye on me the entire time.

"Let me grab Dr. Sebastian." She hurried out of the room.

Was this her way of getting me out of the office? Did she remember but tried to play it off? There were so many things running through my head that I never thought something was actually wrong until the doctor came in.

"June, I'm afraid I'm going to have to put you on bed rest," Dr. Sebastian said, surprising me.

"But I have to work." I gave him the eye so he'd understand what I was saying.

"You won't be working until after the baby comes. You're holding fluid, and your quick urine test shows you've developed high liver enzymes overnight." He was dead serious. "Martha, can you please go get me a new cuff?" He'd wrapped the cuff around my arm to get a blood pressure reading but gave up on the third try. "I think this one is shot."

Martha hurried out of the room.

"Speaking of shot, I've got the files and information that Roma collected to blackmail you. Thank you for getting Martha out of here so we can go over them. She knew a lot." I continued to talk while Dr. Sebastian continued with the fake visit by pretending to listen to my heart and lungs on my back then on my front. "I've got my aunt Helena working on getting it all taken care of. In the meantime—"

"In the meantime, you are on bed rest." He looked up at me with a solemn face.

"You're serious?" I asked since he didn't have an ounce of joking on his face. "I really need to go on bed rest?"

"June, I know you're here because of the Roma thing, but you'd better be glad I got to see you. I'm pretty sure you have preeclampsia, which is a mortal issue where the body rejects the baby."

My heart dropped when I heard "rejects."

"Even though you could give birth to a spiritual baby now, I'm worried with these symptoms, the baby might be mortal."

"Rejects?" I blinked a few times before it all went blank.

CHAPTER TWELVE

"Seester, she's coming to." The familiar voice of Patience Karima made me open my eyes.

"Yes, she is." Constance Karima stood over me. Both of them were, and they were looking at me. "Hi, June. Back to the world, I see."

"Back to the world." Patience nodded.

"What happened?" I pushed myself up on my elbows.

"Take it easy." Constance tried to help me, but she wasn't really steady, so I let her do what she could but really used my own strength. "Patience, go get her a Ding Dong."

"The baby." I immediately put my hand on my belly when I finally remembered I'd been at the doctor's office to talk to Dr. Sebastian about the papers Gus had found in Roma's car—or the stolen car.

"Little One is just fine. You did your fainting thing once you heard the news that the baby could be…" She glanced around before she whispered, "Mortal."

My chin fell to my chest.

"Does Oscar know?" I asked.

"Mm-hmm, he's out in your family room."

She no sooner got the words out than he rushed into the bedroom. "June, you're awake. Are you okay? Are you feeling okay?

The baby?" He peppered me with questions and checked out my ankles.

"I'm fine. I was fine at the doctor's office. I have no inclination that anything is wrong." I sat silently for a few seconds to see if my intuition kicked up anything.

Nothing.

"Did you get the car?" I asked him. "Did you bring him in? To buy us time?"

"*Us* time?" Oscar chuckled. "Even after this." He ran his hand in the air over me. "You still think I'm going to let you even begin to continue to look into a murder? That's probably what put you here. Trying to figure out what happened has made you so stressed out."

After a clap of thunder followed by a cloud of smoke billowing in the bedroom at the foot of my bed, Aunt Helena appeared.

"I'll take over from here," she instructed Oscar. "She and Little One will be just fine."

"It's okay. Give us a minute," I told Oscar when he looked at me for confirmation.

"What is wrong here?" Aunt Helena started in on me before Oscar had even gotten out the door.

I told her what Dr. Sebastian had said about how he thought the baby could be mortal.

"Nonsense," she protested and even took a look at my ankles. "He's proven to be too old to continue as a doctor since I've had to go through his paperwork Gus gave me. I've spent most of my day correcting it all and getting the information you asked Gus to have me get into place."

"The phone number?" I asked.

She nodded.

"The insurance all cleared up?"

She nodded.

"And you think Oscar is going to let me leave this bed?" I still couldn't believe it. I'd yet to tell Oscar that the doctor had told me my condition was a mortal one.

With that piled on top of the murder case, I wasn't sure how much he'd be able to handle. The only thing I knew was that we'd love Little One no matter what.

"Yes. You are the only one that knows the ins and outs of that office. You can do it at night when no one is around." She swung her cloak from around her neck. There was another cloak underneath it. "This is special. It will let anyone who wears it zip in and out, meaning if you put it on tonight, it'll put you right in Dr. Sebastian's reception area. You take it off to do the work, then you put it back on once you have the files set in place."

"I don't know." The tension began to creep up on my forehead. "This whole thing with the swelling of my feet and my body rejecting the baby is something I'm not sure I'd like to put at risk."

"June, as much as I'd love to tell you not to, you are the Chosen One, and you are the only one to stop this from taking down our world." Her eyes narrowed and zeroed in on my stomach. "As for Little One, your plan is fine. I must admit I'm a little concerned, but you and Oscar have turned out fine. I'm sorry I said that about Darla. She was a wonderful wife and mother. I'm forever grateful she was able to keep you safe and leave you with some wisdom in her journal. I might not have agreed at the time, but the time has passed, and it's your time to level up in our world."

Her words were supposed to be comforting, and she was apologizing the best way she knew how, and it was something I was going to have to take at face value.

"So I do it. Then what? There's no caught killer. I don't feel like the boyfriend did it, and I know they brought him in for questioning." I paused when Oscar came into the room.

"Oscar, where do we stand on the boyfriend?" Aunt Helena asked him, putting the cloak back on so he didn't get suspicious.

"We are really talking about this in front of June?" Oscar looked at her like she'd lost her mind. "I'm not doing this here."

"Oscar, I'm fine. I'm in bed, and I need to know what's going on so we can make a plan." I ran my hand down Mr. Prince Charming, who I was sure had never left my side since I'd been passed out.

"June." Oscar looked defeated.

"Please. Aunt Helena might have a solution. She's already gotten the fake insurance offices set up around all the villages. Now we need to know where Dr. Sebastian stands."

I wasn't prepared for what he was about to tell me.

"We went and got the boyfriend on theft charges. The car was exactly how Madame Torres predicted it to be. We also found a gun in the dumpster, hidden in a medical box of some sort. We think it came from inside of the building. The gun matches the ballistics of the bullet that killed Roma," Oscar told us.

"Does that mean they believe the boyfriend did it?" I wasn't following what he was trying to tell me.

"Nope. The gun belongs to the car owner down in Nashville. He has a conceal-and-carry permit, which made the gun licensed and legal. But someone had to know the gun was in the stolen car and turned it on Roma."

He ran his hand through his hair and looked at my belly. I rubbed it and smiled to let him know we were okay.

He continued, "There are no prints on the gun, but what I can tell you is the boyfriend works at the local pizza joint, and he was working at the time of Roma's death. Roma would drop him off in the morning and pick him up after she got off."

"If he has an alibi, what about Martha? What about the letter I over-heard her and Roma discussing?" I asked.

"Martha was home with her family. Roma would often stay later to finish the insurance billing and tidy up before she left because her boyfriend's shift wasn't over. That's why she was at the office. The only other person was Dr. Sebastian."

Oscar had to know there was no way Dr. Sebastian would shoot her. If he had some sort of spiritual gift, he would use that.

"What is his spiritual gift?" I asked.

"He communicates with children. He knows them in the womb, what they are doing, and as little children up until they reach the spiritual legal age," Aunt Helena said. "What does this mean for him?"

"He doesn't have an alibi. Or at least an alibi he can tell us, since he was probably off to a different village or visiting other spiritualists. You're not going to like what else I have to say." He looked between me and Aunt Helena. "Roma's boyfriend told us that Roma was on to some sort of underhanded insurance fraud Dr. Sebastian was involved in. He didn't know the particulars, but she kept telling him how once Dr. Sebastian paid her off, they'd be rich and wouldn't have to run from town to town. So Sonny has called the judge to get a search warrant that'll be served in the morning. If Dr. Sebastian can't produce filings for the insurance, he'll be charged with insurance fraud and probably murder. They are searching everything to see where Roma's claims can be found, because according to her boyfriend, she's got mounting evidence of insurance fraud against the doctor."

"Not having an alibi and now the boyfriend confirming that Roma was looking into something really does make Dr. Sebastian look guilty." Fear ran through my veins.

"Our life, our community, our existence as we know it could come crashing down at any moment." Aunt Helena made me even more jittery. "June would not be at risk, Oscar."

"What do you mean? What will happen?" Oscar asked.

"The end of the spiritual world would be like the end of the world for mortals. The same things would happen. Everything around us would be gray. The clouds would hover, and evil would spread amongst us like a wildfire until we are taken over to death. But June..." She swept her hands out in front of her. "She's part mortal and grew up in a mortal world. She'd survive. There are very few of her kind."

"I grew up in a mortal world." Oscar's voice held desperation.

"You did, but both of your parents were spiritualists, and you were taken from a spiritual village by your uncle. That's the difference." I didn't like how she shifted her eyes to Little One. "Even Little One would be safe if the baby turned out to be a spiritualist, even though the skills aren't fully developed."

Oscar lost all color from his face.

My insides churned. I didn't care what Oscar said. I was going to deliver those files, and I had to save my family.

CHAPTER THIRTEEN

A simple spaghetti-and-meatball dinner with garlic toast was exactly what Oscar needed to fill his belly and get him good and sleepy.

Normally, all those carbs would put me almost into a coma, and Oscar knew that, which I believed was why he made it for supper. What he didn't know was that Little One mainly ate all my carbs up and left me still wanting to eat, but I didn't because I had the mission to complete.

I wanted to say I'd decided to do it for the greater good, but I hadn't. I'd decided to do it for the safety of my family.

Oscar had fallen fast asleep on the couch, and he was doing that open-mouthed snoring thing that told me he was down for a good few hours before he snorted himself awake enough that he'd realize he wasn't in our bed. Then he'd fumble his way back to our bedroom, where the next time he'd wake would be to an alarm.

"Oscar," I called in a normal tone of voice. "Are you awake?"

I had to be sure he didn't hear a thing. I wasn't exactly sure how the cloak that Aunt Helena had stuffed in my bag worked, but I knew it was our only shot.

When Oscar didn't budge, I hurried over to the kitchen chair where my bag was hanging and took the cloak out. The paperwork and files were already secure in my bag, and even Madame Torres was ready to go. I'd be able to use her as a camera into my house so I could check on Oscar.

"This will be easy." I could tell Mr. Prince Charming was going to need some convincing. "We will slip in, put the files back, and zip right back out."

Mr. Prince Charming lay across my feet, feeling like dead weight.

"Stop it. You heard Aunt Helena. We don't have a choice." I reached down, picked him up, and positioned his feet on my belly. Little One went crazy with delight. "I love you, and I've been so grateful for you all these years. This is to save you, Oscar, and Little One. The rest is a bonus, but you're my family. I can't live this life alone if something awful did happen."

He jumped out of my arms and sat next to me, dragging his tail along the floor. I wished he'd do some figure eights to let me know all was good, but he didn't.

"I don't have time for this. The cloak will get me there and back," I told him. With one hand, I drew the cloak over my head, and I clutched my bag with the other.

The light went black. My body had a floating feeling, but I hit a few bumps along the way. It felt like having a bit of turbulence in an airplane.

The clouds below me parted, and I could see Whispering Falls. The fireflies were playing and dotting along the woods where Eloise lived. Locust Grove was quiet, and my little childhood home was dimly lit by the moonlight, making me long for easier times.

Time fell away when I'd lived there. I missed it so much.

Then I turned my sights on the doctor's office. Once again, everything went black, and within the blink of an eye, I stood in the middle of the reception area of Dr. Sebastian's office, exactly like Aunt Helena said I would.

"Let's get to work and get out of here." I dropped the cloak on one of the chairs in the reception area and opened my bag.

The files were already arranged like Aunt Helena had planned, and I just had to get to the office area, where they kept their files.

"Let's do this." I took the files out and rubbed my belly. "But first."

I reached back into my bag and took Madame Torres out.

"Who is it you seek, and who do you wish to seek you?" Madame Torres was wide awake and with a smile on her face. "Nice to see you, June. Up at a good hour, I see."

Her eyes grew, taking up the entire ball. They shifted left then right.

"Where might we be?" she asked.

"We are saving the world. And I seek to see the inside of my house. Specifically Oscar." I tapped her globe.

The globe played like I was watching a television show. Mr. Prince Charming was still next to the table where I'd vanished, being a good fairy god cat and waiting up for me. Oscar was still on the couch with his mouth much wider than before, snoring away.

"We don't have much time before Oscar wakes up." I knew the wider the mouth, the deeper the sleep he was in, and he would soon wake himself up with a snort.

I left Madame Torres along with my bag sitting on the cloak and headed toward the door that led back to the exam rooms and the office space.

There was a shuffling noise coming from Dr. Sebastian's office. I didn't even think about him being there, but of course, where else would he be?

"Dr. Sebastian," I called to him. "Oh." My bracelet gave me a slight sting. "Good news. Aunt Helena doctored the insurance files. I've got them here because the sheriff will be here with a warrant in the morning." I pushed opened the slightly cracked office door.

"A warrant?" Sylvia, Dr. Sebastian's patient, stood at his desk. "What insurance files have been doctored?"

An evil grin curled up on her lips.

"Gosh. I never figured I'd see you here again." Her eyes grew when she emphasized again. "It seems like this world wants us to be involved. But that's not in my plan."

"Plan?" I questioned and tried to get a sense of her spiritual connection, but I couldn't find any. "I'm here to see Dr. Sebastian because I've got preeclampsia, and he wanted to get me tested tonight. My insurance company has approved it."

"Is that right?" she asked and slowly walked around the desk. By the shuffled papers, I could see she'd been going through the desk.

I took a few steps backward as she passed by me, and I noticed a badge clipped on the loops of her pantsuit.

"Rep Pharmaceuticals." I searched my memory for where I'd seen that name. "IVF brochure in the exam room." My face shot up to look at her. Then my intuition kicked in.

I was in danger.

"I see you've connected the two. Me and Rep Pharma." She laughed and shut the office door.

"Why did you shut the door?" I asked.

"I know you're lying. Dr. Sebastian isn't here, and I have no idea what little insurance scheme the two of you have conjured up, but all I want is my cut of the pie, which is why Roma had to go. It's as simple or easy as you want to make it, June Heal." Her smile faltered, her laughter gone. Her eyes narrowed as though she were trying to read me.

I was doing the same as I tried to read her. Glancing away as I tried to figure out what on earth was going on, I noticed a small batch of what looked like test tubes lined up in a holder.

I gasped. "My nightmares. I've been having nightmares about babies not getting food. Not surviving."

"It looks like you've got some sort of psychic ability." She'd noticed I saw the tubes. "You see, Roma and I didn't see eye to eye on the IVF drug Dr. Sebastian was using. I wanted her to use my drug I represent with Rep Pharma, but the rep from Merit Pharmaceuticals was giving Roma a cut of the pie. Which I wouldn't do. I did all the legwork, and I deserve all the money. So when little Roma decided to use her con skills on me, she was conning the wrong person. She refused to let me in to see Dr. Sebastian, and she refused to give him any of my samples. I didn't really know the extent until I did get her out of the way and saw Dr. Sebastian yesterday."

"Why would you kill her? Why wouldn't you get a different doctor?"

"I've got every doctor but him. It was her standing in my way and those little babies over there..." She pointed at the test tubes. "They were ready to be implanted, but I've got them over there, out of the freezer, so they'll die."

"You're killing the embryos?" My heart sank, leaving me paralyzed against the edge of the desk.

"I don't see it as killing. I'm helping the parents get a better product through Dr. Sebastian." Her eyes focused on the files I had pulled up to my chest. "I'm due for a huge raise and a new position with the company. They told me if I landed Dr. Sebastian, since he's the only doctor I've not sold to, they'd give me the position next month. You see, June..." She took a couple steps toward me.

I shifted to the right. She followed. I moved to the left, and she slid to the left. She reached out and put her hands on each side of my belly. Little One went crazy. The baby moved as if it were nervous, knocking into each side of my body and internal organs.

My stomach tightened.

"Oh dear. Maybe I don't have to kill you now that you know my secret. It would be a shame for them to find you dead, bleeding to death with a dead baby."

My eyes followed her eyes down to the ground, where there was a small pool of blood under me.

"Please. Don't do this." I began to beg for my life and the life of Little One. "I just want to put these files back and go home. I'll never breathe a word of it. It's none of my business."

"But you made it your business." She gave an unnerving sigh of happy relief. "Your body is rejecting your unborn baby." She frowned. "And this is what is planned for you. June, nothing happens without a reason. Just like Roma. She had a reason for not using my medical technology, and she died." She threw back her head and laughed. "She, too, begged for her life after I hopped into the passenger side of her car, and lucky me! I popped open the glove box just to get a car registration to see where she lived. I really hadn't planned on killing her, just threatening, but when I saw the gun, boy, did things go south." Sylvia told the story as if she'd had a run of good luck. "It was perfect, actually. Come to find out—the car, she stole it. See, I did the world a favor by getting rid of a common thief."

Her upbeat attitude turned to anger. I held my hands underneath Little One to see if I could stop the baby from moving. My stomach continued to tighten for a few seconds then released.

I bent over in pain.

"Ouuuch!" I cried and threw my head back to catch a breath, still bent over.

"Breathe through it. You're in early labor. But if you don't get the baby out, you'll both die. Your liver enzymes will go up even higher, and your blood pressure will skyrocket. I'm sorry, but this is your fate." She ran her finger along my stomach, and I wanted to smack it away so much, but the pain coursed through every muscle in my body, sending me to the ground.

"Little One," I whispered, trying to calm the baby and me, "please, please hold on." Sweat beads formed along my brow. "It's going to be okay." I rolled over to my other side in agony to face the door and to see where Sylvia was.

Her feet were practically touching my nose. I glanced up to see her standing over me with a satisfied look on her face.

"Not all of us can have natural babies and pregnancies," she began, telling her personal story while I lay there. "I never lied to you about how many miscarriages I had."

I stared at the door, trying to breathe through the pain. Four little white paws appeared under the crack. I closed my eyes and sighed in relief.

"Did you ever think you miscarried because those sweet, innocent babies didn't want an evil mother like you?" I mustered up the worst comment I could give her.

"Why, you little. . ." She grabbed Dr. Sebastian's nameplate off of his desk and put it over her head like she was going to bring it down on me.

"Hold it right there!" Oscar kicked in the door and stood with his Locust Grove sheriff's uniform on, his gun directly aimed at her. "You are under arrest for the murder of Roma Klein. And I'm not sure, but I think I can arrest you on murder charges for those embryos too."

CHAPTER FOURTEEN

Everything that happened after Oscar saved me and Little One was practically a blur. Somehow, they'd gotten me to one of the exam rooms, where Eloise was standing next to the table. Her short red hair was bright and sunny. It made me happy to see her. She had on an apron and a pair of gloves.

"Now, now," she said to me and rubbed her gloved hand over my head. The beads of sweat kept my bangs off my face. "You can stop crying. Everything will be okay."

In that instance, I knew it was Eloise who was going to actually save the day and deliver Little One.

"You're the chosen deliverer?" I questioned as she moved her hands down to Little One and began to press really hard on my stomach.

"Yes. Darla had it in the journal, and you secretly desired it. Now breathe through it as we meet our Little One." Her words soothed me and made me feel secure.

The pain eased right in time for Oscar to come in and rush to me, giving me the strength to talk to him.

"Madame Torres," I whispered.

"I'll get her." He hurried out the room.

"Push, June!" Eloise's voice boomed in my ear. "June, push now!" she yelled.

I tried with all my might to push. Nothing.

I looked down at Eloise. She put a limp smile on her face, but I saw concern in her eyes. Oscar came in and sat Madame Torres on the counter.

"You did well. Getting closer." Her words were nothing but letters put together. I could hear it in her voice that something was wrong.

"Can I talk to you in private?" she asked Oscar. "We will be right back, June."

There was no reason for me to ask what was happening. I knew. I'd put myself and Little One in danger by trying to save everyone else.

The tears dropped down my face as I tried to make sense of my life and who I was. I was an outsider in my own world. Though I had been taken in and given a warm home in Whispering Falls, I was still an outsider as my half mortal world collided with the spiritual world.

Madame Torres glowed a light pink. I watched the waves move slowly in and around the glass globe while I took long, deep breaths.

"Everything that you desire is within reach, waiting for you to recognize your own power. You are courageous. You are capable. You are whole. You are powerful." The words floated bright white as a pair of lips read them.

I knew those lips. Those lips had kissed my boo-boos on my skinned knees. They gave me words of comfort when I was heart-broken as a teenager. Those lips sang happy birthday to me. Those lips told me they loved me. Those lips belonged to Darla.

I ran my hand over my charm bracelet and knew the elephant charm Mr. Prince Charming had given me a few days ago was from Darla.

"June." Oscar came in. His eyes were red, and his face was blotchy.

"Tell Eloise I'm ready." I refused to believe she'd told him something was wrong and things weren't going to turn out.

"June, we need to talk." Oscar was determined to tell me.

"No, we don't. I'm going to have a baby. Right now, go get Eloise."

With everything I could muster, I pulled myself up and grabbed my knees.

Eloise ran in and looked me over.

"Move it." She knocked Oscar out of the way. She gave me an assured look. "Are you ready now?"

"Yes." I smiled and gave a few final pushes.

I wouldn't say they were easy. They certainly weren't, and the pain was pretty unbelievable. But I'd not come so far to save the spiritual world not to bring another spiritual baby into it.

"One final push should do it." I totally focused on what Eloise was saying and did exactly what she said.

The sound of a baby crying loudly rang out into the exam room. Oscar cried out in joy as he looked at the crying baby Eloise was cleaning up.

I laid my head back with a sigh of relief. The baby was here.

"Congratulations, Mom." Oscar walked up to my head and handed me the swaddled baby. "We have a girl."

"A girl?" I teared up and knew the light-pink waves in Madame Torres's ball were Darla's way of encouraging me and letting me know everything was okay and she was here.

CHAPTER FIFTEEN

"Baby Lo." Adeline put her hands out and did the gimme gesture. "I love her," she gushed.

"How did you get the name?" Petunia asked and tugged on the dog leash she had attached to Orin.

"Oscar and I thought it was fitting since we always referred to the baby as Little One. *L* for little. *O* for one." I put a piece of the baby shower cake into my mouth and savored every single morsel of the June's Gem in cake form.

"How are you feeling?" Petunia asked me.

"I'm good. I've come to terms with the fact that I honestly just want to have a family and work as a spiritualist." I looked around at our group of spiritual friends who'd gathered for the baby shower, which was supposed to be before Lo arrived, but things had changed, as we all knew.

The pink-and-white helium balloons floated in the air without being tied to anything. There were pink flowers in pink vases all over. Pink wildflowers covered the ground as far as the eye could see.

Mr. Prince Charming even had on a pink bow tie. He had not left Lo's side since she'd made her big debut into the world. Many times, it made me pause, because there was no feeling of him protecting me.

He darted between the women as they passed Lo around. Each one took their time with her and whispered deep secrets into her precious ears—secrets that I was sure were about the spiritual world and her role to be played, even though we wouldn't know what her gift would be until she was well into her teen years.

"Petunia, you really need to get Orin into childcare at Hidden Hall." Aunt Helena had been keeping a close eye on Orin since she'd gotten there. "I have the perfect room just for him, where we can help refine the skills you've given him."

"That sounds wonderful. Can you start tomorrow?" There was a bit of relief on Petunia's face that told me she was ready to get some help with him.

While she and Aunt Helena talked, I walked over to the Karima sisters and picked up Lo.

It was time for her nap, and she'd be perfectly fine in the bassinette I'd just opened while we finished the baby shower.

Mr. Prince Charming trotted next to me.

"You love her as much as I do." I ran a hand along his back. He did figure eights around my ankles when I bent over and put Lo in the sleeper. "You're such a good boy."

Mr. Prince Charming jumped into Lo's bassinette. Both of us stared at the beautiful baby.

"What's that?" I asked Mr. Prince Charming when he dropped something next to Lo's head in her bassinette.

"June, I'm sorry I'm late." Bella held out a small box. "For Lo."

When I opened it, I pulled out a small charm bracelet. The tiniest of chains I'd ever seen had links on it.

A twinkle next to Lo's head caught my eye, and I noticed it was a small turtle charm with one little emerald-green eye. The other one was missing.

My jaw dropped as I started to put the clues together.

"Yes, June. You now have only one familiar." Bella laughed.

"Don't tell me it's Madame Torres," I joked, knowing Lo had her very own Mr. Prince Charming, who would protect her even if I wasn't there.

Actually, it was perfect. Everything was perfect. Dr. Sebastian had been cleared of fraud and killing Roma. The things Aunt Helena had put into place for the insurance were perfect and ran smoothly. Martha was back at work as Dr. Sebastian's nurse, and Faith Mortimer took on the administrative role on the days I didn't need her to babysit Lo.

"Hey there." Oscar walked up behind me and gave me a kiss on my cheek. He handed me another piece of June's Gems cake.

Lo started to wiggle around and began to cry.

Oscar reached in and picked her up. He noticed the charm bracelet on Lo's wrist. He glanced at me and smiled.

"So that's why Mr. Prince Charming hasn't left her side?" Oscar asked, and I nodded.

Lo started to fuss. I held my arms out.

"I've got her," he insisted and cuddled her to him to free up an arm.

He used his finger to swipe a piece of the June's Gems cake and let Lo try to suck it off his finger. She smiled and cooed, looking up at him.

"Like mother, like daughter." Oscar beamed with deep love in his eyes.

Stay tuned for the next book in the series! A Charming Hexocist coming soon!

. . .

BUT WAIT! Readers ask me how much my cozy mysteries and the characters in them reflect my real life. Well…here is a good story for you.

WHOOO HOOO!! I'm so glad we are a week out from last Coffee Chat with Tonya and happy to report the poison ivy is almost gone! But y'all we got more issues than Time magazine up in our family.

When y'all ask me if my real life ever creeps into books, well…grab your coffee because here is a prime example!

My sweet mom's birthday was over the weekend. Now, I'd already decided me and Rowena was going to stay there for a couple of extra days.

On her birthday, Sunday, Tracy and David were there too, and we were talking about what else…poison ivy! I was telling them how I can't stand not shaving my legs. Mom and Tracy told me they don't shave daily and I might've curled my nose a smidgen. And apparently it didn't go unnoticed.

I went inside the house to start cooking breakfast for everyone and mom went up to her room to get her bathing suit on and Tracy was with me. All the men were already outside on the porch.

The awfulest crash came from upstairs and my sister tore out of that kitchen like a bat out of hell and I kept flipping the bacon. My mom had fallen…shaving her legs!

Great. Now it's my fault.

Her wrist was a little stiff but she kept saying she was fine. We had a great day. We celebrated her birthday, swam, and had cake. When it came time for everyone to leave but me and Ro, I told mom that she should probably go get an x-ray because her wrist was a little swollen.

After a lot of coaxing, she agreed and I put my shoes on and told Tracy, David, and Eddy to go on home and we'd call them.

My mama looked me square in the face and said, "You're going with that top knot on your head?"

I said, "yes."

She sat back down in the chair and said, "I'm not going with you lookin' like that."

"Are you serious?" I asked.

"Yes. I'm dead serious. I'm not going with you looking like that. What if we see someone?" She was serious, y'all!

She protested against my hair!

Now...this is exactly like the southern mama's I write about! I looked at Eddy and he was laughing. Tracy and David were laughing and I said, "I can't wait until I tell my coffee chat people about this."

As you can see in the above photo, the before and after photo.

Yep...we went and she broke her wrist! Can you believe that? We were a tad bit shocked, and I'll probably be staying a few extra days (which will give us even more to talk about over coffee next week).

Oh...we didn't see anyone we knew so I could've worn my top knot! As I'm writing this, you can bet your bottom dollar my hair is pulled up in my top knot!

Okay, so y'all might be asking why I'm putting this little story in the back of my book, well, that's a darn tootin' good question.

This is exactly what you can expect when you sign up for my newsletter. There's always something going on in my life that I have to chat with y'all about each Tuesday on Coffee Chat with Tonya. Go to Tonyakappes.com and click on subscribe in the upper right corner to join.

If you enjoyed reading this book as much as I enjoyed writing it then be sure to return to the Amazon page and leave a review.

Go to Tonyakappes.com for a full reading order of my novels and while there join my newsletter. You can also find links to Facebook, Instagram and Goodreads.

Join like-minded readers like YOU in the Cozy Krew Facebook Group for dream casting, fan theories, and live Q & A's. It's like a BIG GIANT BOOK CLUB! But if you want to have your own book club, be sure you let me know! I love to send goodies.

Also By Tonya Kappes

A Camper and Criminals Cozy Mystery
BEACHES, BUNGALOWS, & BURGLARIES
DESERTS, DRIVERS, & DERELICTS
FORESTS, FISHING, & FORGERY
CHRISTMAS, CRIMINALS, & CAMPERS
MOTORHOMES, MAPS, & MURDER
CANYONS, CARAVANS, & CADAVERS
HITCHES, HIDEOUTS, & HOMICIDE
ASSAILANTS, ASPHALT, & ALIBIS
VALLEYS, VEHICLES & VICTIMS
SUNSETS, SABBATICAL, & SCANDAL
TENTS, TRAILS, & TURMOIL
KICKBACKS, KAYAKS, & KIDNAPPING
GEAR, GRILLS, & GUNS
EGGNOG, EXTORTION, & EVERGREENS
ROPES, RIDDLES, & ROBBERIES
PADDLERS, PROMISES, & POISON
INSECTS, IVY, & INVESTIGATIONS
OUTDOORS, OARS, & OATHS
WILDLIFE, WARRANTS, & WEAPONS
BLOSSOMS, BARBEQUE, & BLACKMAIL
LANTERNS, LAKES, & LARCENY
JACKETS, JACK-O-LANTERN, & JUSTICE
SANTA, SUNRISES, & SUSPICIONS
VISTAS, VICES, & VALENTINES
ADVENTURE, ABDUCTION, & ARREST
RANGERS, RV'S, & REVENGE
CAMPFIRES, COURAGE, & CONVICTS
TRAPPING, TURKEYS, & THANKSGIVING
GIFTS, GLAMPING, & GLOCKS
ZONING, ZEALOTS, & ZIPLINES

HAMMOCKS, HANDGUNS, & HEARSAY

Kenni Lowry Mystery Series
FIXIN' TO DIE
SOUTHERN FRIED
AX TO GRIND
SIX FEET UNDER
DEAD AS A DOORNAIL
TANGLED UP IN TINSEL
DIGGIN' UP DIRT
BLOWIN' UP A MURDER

Killer Coffee Mystery Series
SCENE OF THE GRIND
MOCHA AND MURDER
FRESHLY GROUND MURDER
COLD BLOODED BREW
DECAFFEINATED SCANDAL
A KILLER LATTE
HOLIDAY ROAST MORTEM
DEAD TO THE LAST DROP
A CHARMING BLEND NOVELLA (CROSSOVER WITH MAGICAL
CURES MYSTERY)
FROTHY FOUL PLAY
SPOONFUL OF MURDER
BARISTA BUMP-OFF
CAPPUCCINO CRIMINAL

Holiday Cozy Mystery
FOUR LEAF FELONY
MOTHER'S DAY MURDER
A HALLOWEEN HOMICIDE
NEW YEAR NUISANCE
CHOCOLATE BUNNY BETRAYAL

APRIL FOOL'S ALIBI
FATHER'S DAY MURDER
THANKSGIVING TREACHERY
SANTA CLAUSE SURPRISE

Mail Carrier Cozy Mystery
STAMPED OUT
ADDRESS FOR MURDER
ALL SHE WROTE
RETURN TO SENDER
FIRST CLASS KILLER
POST MORTEM
DEADLY DELIVERY
RED LETTER SLAY

Magical Cures Mystery Series
A CHARMING CRIME
A CHARMING CURE
A CHARMING POTION (novella)
A CHARMING WISH
A CHARMING SPELL
A CHARMING MAGIC
A CHARMING SECRET
A CHARMING CHRISTMAS (novella)
A CHARMING FATALITY
A CHARMING DEATH (novella)
A CHARMING GHOST
A CHARMING HEX
A CHARMING VOODOO
A CHARMING CORPSE
A CHARMING MISFORTUNE
A CHARMING BLEND (CROSSOVER WITH A KILLER COFFEE COZY)
A CHARMING DECEPTION

A Southern Magical Bakery Cozy Mystery Serial
A SOUTHERN MAGICAL BAKERY

A Ghostly Southern Mystery Series
A GHOSTLY UNDERTAKING
A GHOSTLY GRAVE
A GHOSTLY DEMISE
A GHOSTLY MURDER
A GHOSTLY REUNION
A GHOSTLY MORTALITY
A GHOSTLY SECRET
A GHOSTLY SUSPECT

A Southern Cake Baker Series
(WRITTEN UNDER MAYEE BELL)
CAKE AND PUNISHMENT
BATTER OFF DEAD

Spies and Spells Mystery Series
SPIES AND SPELLS
BETTING OFF DEAD
GET WITCH or DIE TRYING

A Laurel London Mystery Series
CHECKERED CRIME
CHECKERED PAST
CHECKERED THIEF

A Divorced Diva Beading Mystery Series
A BEAD OF DOUBT SHORT STORY
STRUNG OUT TO DIE
CRIMPED TO DEATH

Olivia Davis Paranormal Mystery Series

About Tonya

Tonya has written over 100 novels, all of which have graced numerous bestseller lists, including the USA Today. *Best known for stories charged with emotion and humor and filled with flawed characters, her novels have garnered reader praise and glowing critical reviews. She lives with her husband and a very spoiled rescue cat named Ro. Tonya grew up in the small southern Kentucky town of Nicholasville. Now that her four boys are grown men, Tonya writes full-time in her camper she calls her SHAMPER (she-camper).*

Learn more about her be sure to check out her website tonyakappes.com. Find her on Facebook, Twitter, BookBub, and Instagram

Sign up to receive her newsletter, where you'll get free books, exclusive bonus content, and news of her releases and sales.

If you liked this book, please take a few minutes to leave a review now! Authors (Tonya included) really appreciate this, and it helps draw more readers to books they might like. Thanks!

Cover artist: Mariah Sinclair: The Cover Vault

Milton Keynes UK
Ingram Content Group UK Ltd.
UKHW021307010923
427900UK00023B/561

9 781708 412791